Vote for the Class Acts couple
you'd like to read about next...

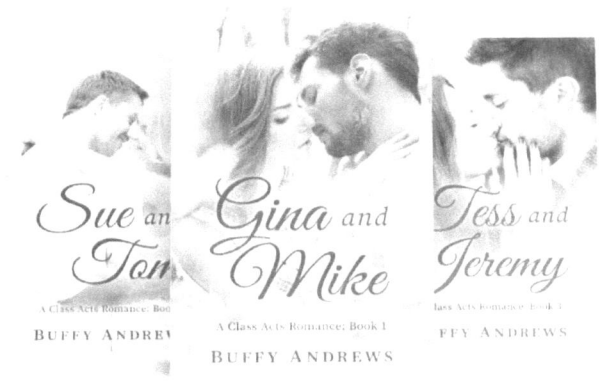

Kris and Keith

Cookie and Harry

Maggie and James

Karen and Mia

Cast your vote at http://bit.ly/35zdR9n

Also by Buffy Andrews

Samuel's Secret

The Perfect Husband

The Moment Keeper

The Christmas Violin

The Stone Giver

A Year of Second Chances

Our Fragile Hearts

It's in the Stars

Ella's Rain

The Lion Awakens

Tess and Jeremy

Class Acts

BUFFY ANDREWS

Andrews Creative Concepts
York, Pennsylvania 17404
andrewscreativeconcepts.com

Print ISBN: 978-1-7352216-6-3
Ebook ISBN: 978-1-7352216-7-0

First edition 2014, The Yearbook Series
Second edition 2020, Class Acts
Published in the United States of America

To Robin and Kris, my BFFs.
I love you girls so much!

Chapter 1

Jeremy

I never saw it coming. I thought Tess was happy. I thought I'd given her a good life. I didn't know she was checking out until she was half way out the door. And I hoped I could stop her before she closed it for good.

It started with little things. Like I noticed she was losing weight. Not that she was fat, but after a couple of kids she had more around the middle than when we were married fourteen years ago. I still thought she was as sexy as hell. And I told her that. But I could feel her pulling away more each day.

I couldn't figure out what I was doing wrong. I tried complimenting her more, but that only seemed to piss her off. "You're just saying that to make me feel better," she'd say.

She complained I didn't do enough around the house, but when I tried doing more, it was never right. And sex? Don't even get me started. I've never been priest material. When I met Tess in dental school, we screwed every chance we got. We even did it on the dental chair once!

But now? Now I'm lucky to get it once a month, and I'm horny as hell. I'm trying to be understanding, give her some space. I thought maybe she was in some kind of funk. But when my buddy Keith told me about his wife, Kris, and him doing the deed for 31 days straight,

I became worried. And then when he told me about Kris dabbing chocolate five different places on her body and him having to find the five places and lick off the chocolate while blindfolded, I *really* became worried. My sex life—er marriage—was in a definite nosedive, and I'll be damned if I knew how to stop it from crashing.

When I came home from work, I found Tess in the kitchen making dinner. "How was your day?"

She didn't look up from slicing carrots for the salad she was making. "Same as yesterday."

I grabbed a beer from the refrigerator. "I thought you had parent visitation at Katie's school."

"I did."

"How'd that go?"

"Fine."

I sipped my beer. "Not in the mood to talk?"

Tess scooped up the carrot slices and tossed them into the salad bowl. "I want to talk, but you don't want to hear what I have to say."

"Come on, Tess. That's not fair. I always listen to what you have to say."

This time she looked up at me, her twitching eyes boring into mine. "Okay. I want to go back to work."

I wiped my mouth with the back of my hand. "But we talked about this."

Tess narrowed her eyes. "You talked. I tried to talk, but you didn't listen."

"I just don't see why you want to get a job when you don't have to. You can golf at the country club anytime you want. Go shopping every day if you want. You have more time for yourself now than you ever did with both kids in school and not needing you as much. Most women would kill to have your life."

Tess threw the dish towel she'd been holding onto the counter. "You just don't get it, do you? I'm not like most women!"

I drank the last sip of my beer as she flew up the stairs. I heard our bedroom door slam shut.

Tess

I knew I had to calm down. Jeremy made my blood boil, and I didn't want to get into another fight. It seemed as if that's all we did anymore. Fight, fight, fight! And fight some more! I couldn't remember the last time Jeremy came home from work and we had a normal conversation. Usually within five minutes of him getting home our conversation deteriorates into a screaming match. I was beginning to feel as if I lived in a war zone, and all of the yelling wasn't good for the kids. Just this morning Katie asked if her dad and I were getting a divorce. Of course I said no, but I found myself thinking about the possibility more and more. I just couldn't make Jeremy understand I wanted to go back to work.

When the kids were younger and needed me more, I had no problem not working outside the home. In fact, I enjoyed the stay-at-home momminess and everything that came with it—story time at the library and days spent at the park or pool. But they're in third and fifth grade, old enough to walk home from the bus stop, fix an afternoon snack and do their homework with the help of a babysitter.

I loved being Katie's and John's mom, but I wanted more than to be their mom. I wanted a career I could feel good about. I wanted the pre-mom me, and damn if I could get that through Jeremy's brick brain. I couldn't seem to make him understand I needed to have something that made me feel good about myself, something outside the family and home that was all mine. I wasn't exactly sure what it would be, but I want to explore and find out.

And the more Jeremy resisted, the more I pulled away. I focused on other things that made me feel good—like getting in shape. At least *that* was something I had control over. And I had no interest in having sex with him. I felt so misunderstood and alone. I'd be willing to go to counseling, but I wasn't sure Jeremy would. He didn't like other people knowing our business.

I heard a knock on the door. I knew it was Jeremy. "Go away!"

Jeremy cracked open the door. "Can I come in?"

"Only if you'll listen. If you're not going to listen, don't bother."

He walked in and closed the door.

"So, you really think getting a job will make you happier?"

I clenched my teeth. "That's what I've been saying."

Jeremy sat down on the bed next to me. "My mom didn't work, and she was happy."

I stared into the dark eyes that once melted me in seconds. "Well, I'm not your mom."

"People might think I'm not a good provider?"

"Jesus! Are you serious? You're really worried about that shit! Get over it. I don't give a damn what anyone thinks. This isn't about you being a good provider. This is about me wanting a job so I feel useful and good about myself."

"But what if the kids get sick?"

4

"Your mom has always offered to help out anytime. You just never wanted to ask her."

Jeremy rubbed his neck. "Well, we sure can't continue fighting like this. Even the dog crawls under the sofa whenever we're in the same room."

"Look, Jeremy. I've decided I'm going to get a job whether you like it or not. Now, I'm really hoping you'll support me. But if you don't, I'll do it anyway."

"But the wash and cleaning and all the other stuff."

"What about it?"

"Who's going to do it if you work?"

"Guess we'll have to do like most married couples and split the jobs."

Jeremy punched the bed. "I work long days at the office, and the last thing I want to do is come home and make dinner."

"Then find someone else to make it for you."

I stormed out of the bedroom and went to the kitchen to finish making the kids dinner. As far as Jeremy was concerned, he could just go fuck himself. I've had it.

Jeremy

Damn Tess. I don't want my life to change. I like coming home from work and having dinner on the table. I like knowing the kids are taken care of, the house is clean and the laundry done. And the last thing I want is for her to change all that. I did an informal poll at work and every woman in my dental office said if given the chance, she'd choose staying home over working. But no! Not my wife.

My best friend, Mike, suggested marriage counseling. But I'm not crazy about sharing all this personal stuff with a therapist. Besides, I think we can fix what's wrong ourselves. I suggested to Tess she volunteer more at the school, but she says if she volunteers anymore the teachers will get sick of seeing her.

When we married, Tess was a graphic artist for an advertising company. Later, she became art director for a regional women's magazine. She loved that job, but decided to stay home when we had John. Her mother had always worked, and Tess said she always envied the kids whose moms were waiting for them at the end of the school day. She was happy for a while, but little by little, I could see she was becoming restless. Katie's birth changed things for a while, but now we've come full circle.

I went downstairs to see if I could help with dinner, but Tess and the kids were already eating. Katie, who looked like a miniature Tess with black hair and violet eyes, looked up at me. "Why do you and Mom fight all the time?"

I patted her on the head before sitting down. "We don't, sweetie."

"Do, too," John chimed in. "We heard you. Upstairs."

Katie nodded. "Yeah, Mom said 'Jesus' and we learned in Sunday school you're not supposed to say that when you're mad. You're supposed to say it only when you pray."

I looked at Tess who was mashing her lips together so hard they were turning blue.

"I'm sorry, Katie," I said. "You're right. We shouldn't have said that."

"And you shouldn't have said 'damn' either," John added.

I looked at John. "That, too."

Tess and I didn't talk much during dinner. Mostly we listened to the kids talk about their day.

Tess

When Katie mentioned she overheard me say Jesus, I realized the kids were tuned into what had been going on far more than I realized.

"How was your practice spelling test today?" I asked Katie during dinner.

She jabbed a carrot slice with her fork. "Okay. I got one wrong."

"Which one?"

"Vocal. I put two *l*'s at the end."

John pointed to me and Jeremy. "That's what you guys were when you were upstairs. Vocal."

Katie smiled. "Thanks, John. I can use that when I write my sentences. Mom and Dad are vocal when they fight."

I coughed. "Oh, Katie. I'm sure you can come up with a better sentence than that."

Katie shook her head. "I like that sentence. It's perfect."

I looked across the table at Jeremy, and he rolled his eyes. "Remember tomorrow night, Tess. We're going to Tom's house for dinner."

Katie rubbed her hands together. "Is Cassie going to babysit us?"

I nodded. I was actually looking forward to seeing Gina and Sue and the other girls. I really liked them, and I thought they might be able to give me some advice on how to handle Jeremy.

I'd been going to the gym a lot lately, and the manager, who's also a kick-ass instructor, asked if I'd ever considered teaching classes. I hadn't, but the more I thought about it, the more interested I became.

Chapter 2

Jeremy

When I crawled into bed that night, I felt as if I'd climbed into a deep freezer. Tess was as far to the side of our king bed as she could get without falling out. There was a time when our bodies interlocked like two puzzle pieces. A crowbar wouldn't have been able to pry us apart. Damn! I miss those nights.

I knew she was awake, but she didn't say anything. It had become our nightly routine. I was lonely and horny. I wanted to hold her in my arms, feel her skin against mine. Our recent conversations—er fights— flooded my mind—Tess wanting to work, me wanting her to stay home, Tess telling me to fuck off, that she was going to find a job whether I liked it or not. The divide between us was growing exponentially.

I had to admit I admired her spunkiness. It was one of the reasons I fell in love with her. But when I thought about it, I hadn't seen a lot of that spunkiness in recent years. It had sort of died—like our marriage. And I kind of wondered if I'd killed it. Or if that's what happens in life?

Everything seemed to change after we had kids. They took center stage, and I was left standing in the wing. I'd never admit this to anyone, but it sort of bothered me. I liked being the most important person in Tess's life, and I wasn't anymore. Over the years, she had less and less time for me. I guess that's how it is when you have kids, but I wasn't happy and I knew Tess wasn't either. Somehow we had to find each other again, get back what we'd lost. But hell if I knew how.

I even googled "romantic ideas for men" and made a list of ones I wanted to try. I figured at this point I had nothing to lose.

I lay in bed, thinking about the first time I saw Tess. It was at a dive bar around the corner from the university we attended. She was standing across the smoky room with a few friends. They were laughing and having a good time. She was as sexy as hell. Her long black hair fanned her back. Her eyes caught mine, and she flashed her gorgeous smile. I worked my way over to where she stood and blurted the lamest pick up line ever.

"You have great teeth."

She shook her head. "What?"

Her puzzled look made me feel like a complete ass. "I'm sorry. That was really stupid, wasn't it?"

She shrugged. "I've heard worse."

I felt the need to explain. "I'm in dental school, so, you know, I notice teeth—a lot."

She smiled. "In that case I'll give you a pass."

And we talked the rest of the night, and I walked her back to her dorm. And I saw her the next night and the next. And the rest is history, as they say.

I heard Jeremy open the bedroom door so I wiggled as far over to the edge of the bed as I could. I didn't want him touching me. I was too mad.

"Tess, I know you're awake," Jeremy whispered.

"I am not."

"Can we talk?

"No. My mouth's tired of talking."

Jeremy sighed. "Damn it, Tess. You agreed when we had kids you'd stay at home. Now, you want to change the game plan. I didn't sign up for that."

"Jeremy, fuck off. I didn't sign up to have an asshole for a husband."

Jeremy punched the bed. I felt him get up, grab his pillow and leave. I knew he was heading to the guest bedroom. He closed the door, and I laid awake thinking about our crappy marriage. I blamed myself. After all, if I would've continued to be content not working outside the home, none of this would've happened. But I wasn't, so it did.

I remembered holding John in my arms for the first time. He was the most beautiful baby I'd ever seen. He had tiny hands and tiny feet and a tiny head topped with a tuft of fine black hair. I was so afraid he wouldn't get enough to eat or I'd screw something up while taking care of him. I felt the same way when Katie was born. She was even tinier, and the way her straw fingers grasped mine I thought she'd need me forever.

But time has a way of loosening those fingers. It's not that I don't think they need me anymore. I know they do. But they don't need me every minute of every day. There's time to do things I want to do—and what I want to do is work.

I suppose I'd spoiled Jeremy over the years. He never had to worry about the kids or our home. He only had to worry about work. And now I was asking him to shoulder some of the load so I could work, too. It seemed like either he was going to be miserable or I was, and I wondered if there was any way we could both be happy again.

Jeremy

I couldn't remember the last time Tess and I made love. She was either too pissed or too full or too bloated or too tired. And I was too horny to fall asleep. I thought about going back over and apologizing. If I knew I would end up getting laid, I would. But I knew it would take more than an apology at this point to set things straight.

Things weren't much better in the morning.

"Are you and Mom still fighting?" asked Katie when I walked into the kitchen.

John looked up from reading his comic book. "He slept in the guest bedroom last night. What does that tell you?"

Katie nodded. "Still fighting."

"All right, kids. That's enough," I said. "Mom and I are just having a little disagreement."

"And you're vocal about it," said Katie, smiling.

Tess looked up from packing Katie's lunch. "You should practice your other spelling words, Katie. What else is on your list?"

"Brother. My brother's dumb."

"Am not."

"Are too."

"Stop it," I said. "No one's dumb. John, eat your cereal. And Katie, finish your toast. And don't look or talk to each other."

I sat down to drink my coffee and look at the newspaper. Tess finished making Katie's lunch and sat down, too.

"Anything fun planned today?" I asked Tess.

The kids looked at Tess, probably waiting to see if she was going to answer nicely or fire a smart comeback.

"Probably go to the gym. Not sure about after that."

I got up to pour another cup of coffee. "It'll be nice seeing the gang tonight."

"Yeah, I'm anxious to see how big Gina is. And Cookie's always a hoot."

"I haven't been to Tom's since Sue moved in," I said. "I think Tom finally has the girl he's always wanted."

"Good for him. And her. I love happy endings."

John and Katie went to brush their teeth.

I took a sip of my coffee. "Do you think we'll have a happy ending?"

Tess shrugged. "I don't know."

The kids rushed down the stairs, and Tess got up to see them out the door. The bus stop was at the end of the block. When she returned, I was putting my coffee mug in the dishwasher. "If you want to work, work. We'll figure things out. I'm tired of all the fighting."

Tess

I guess I should be happy Jeremy said I could work. But it bugged me. I didn't want his permission. I wanted his support. I wanted him to understand why I wanted to work, not agree to it because he wants to get laid. And believe me, I know when he wants to get laid. He's as horny as a guy at a single women's convention.

I hit every red light on the way to the gym and slipped into cycling class just as they finished the first song. There was a seat in the back next to this hunk of a guy who attracted more women than a shoe sale. And judging by the way the women talked about him in the locker room, most of them—married or not—would do him in a second if he was interested. But he never was. At least that's what those who've tried have said. Some even wondered if he might be gay.

It didn't take me long to warm up and get into the groove. Maggie was a tough instructor. We called her Maniac Maggie, and for good reason.

"Come on, people," she shouted. "Get those legs moving. Faster. This isn't supposed to be a leisurely ride around the neighborhood. Imagine being on a flat stretch of road and going as fast as you can. Now pick it up!"

I did what Maggie said and pictured being on a flat road; I pedaled as fast as I could. My heart raced. Sweat dripped off my face and onto the bike and floor. When the song was over, I reached for my water bottle to take a sip.

"Good job," Maniac Maggie shouted. "Now, it's time for the hill. When I tell you to, add resistance, a little at a time. By the time we get to the top of the hill, you'll have to stand to pedal!"

I heard Hillary, who sat in front of me, sigh. She's one of those women who comes to the gym to gawk at guys. She admits she hates working out and thinks sweating is gross, but she comes for the eye candy.

The hill was a killer, and by the time class was over I felt like I'd been through SEAL Training Hell Week.

Maggie totally whipped my ass. The air was heavy with sweat, and I could barely stand smelling myself. I jumped off the bike and wiped it off.

"Tough class today, huh?"

I looked up, and Hunky Guy was talking to me.

I sighed. "All of Maggie's classes are tough."

He smiled. "Guess that's true. I'm Cole, by the way."

Normally, I'd have shaken his hand, but I really didn't want to shake his sweaty hand, so I flicked a little wave instead. "I'm Teresa. My friends call me Tess."

"Nice to meet you, Tess. I've seen you around. You take your workouts seriously. Not like, you know, some of the other women here."

"Thanks, I guess."

I didn't like how my heart fluttered, and it wasn't fluttering from the adrenaline surge from class. It was fluttering because of Cole. I hadn't really noticed before, not in the way Hillary and the other women had, but he was a perfect male specimen. And nice, too.

"Well, I have to hit the shower. It was nice meeting you, Cole."

"You, too, Tess. Maybe I'll see you around."

See you around? What did that mean? I definitely didn't like how this man was making me go all liquid. My face flooded with heat, and I made a beeline to the shower to cool off. As I walked out the door, I noticed Hillary was eye banging Cole. She could be a little less obvious, I thought. I never saw anyone moan with her eyes the way she does. She was one horny woman.

I jumped in the shower but couldn't stop thinking about Cole. I wasn't sure why he had affected me so. I mean, he had to be at least ten years younger, which would put him at 28. I'm sure he wasn't married, but I wondered if he had a girlfriend.

Damn! Why am I even thinking about this guy? I'm married. I have kids. But the electricity I felt I knew he felt, too. I could see it in his eyes, and it spooked me. I didn't like what I was thinking, and I needed to make sure my thoughts stayed just thoughts. And that I could stop thinking them.

Chapter 3

Jeremy

I was glad the work week was over. I looked forward to the party at Tom and Sue's. It was hard to believe how fast things happened between them. It seemed like only yesterday they had reconnected at our 20th class reunion, and now they were living together. They seemed really happy, too. Unlike me and Tess who at the moment could be poster children for failing marriages.

I was getting dressed in the bedroom when Tess walked in fresh from a shower. God, she was beautiful. I could tell by her toned body and the definition in her arms and legs she'd been working out. She looked even better than she had in college, and I never would've figured on that happening—especially after two kids.

She slid on a pair of jeans and a white shirt with a plunging neckline that hugged her, showing off her figure. I wanted to make love to her, but I was afraid to even try.

"You look nice," I said.

She stuck an earring in her ear. "Thanks."

"Should we stop at the store to pick up a bottle or two of wine to take?"

She leaned toward her vanity mirror, stopping inches from it. She slightly parted her lips and rolled lipstick over the top lip and then the bottom. Then she rubbed her lips together and checked the mirror again. "Already bought the wine. And made a dessert."

"So we're good to go?"

"Yes, as soon as Cassie gets here."

The doorbell rang.

"Sounds like she's here," said Tess, and left to greet her.

I looked in the mirror, trying to decide if I needed to shave. Oh, what the hell. I didn't feel like it and it wasn't that bad. Besides, there was a time Tess liked me on the scruffy side. Said it kind of reminded her of a bad boy. Maybe she'd let me be her bad boy tonight.

When I got downstairs, Katie already had Cassie making some sort of rubber band bracelets and John was parked in front of the flat screen playing a video game.

"You know the routine," Tess told Cassie. "I left our numbers on the notepad on the counter." She looked at the kids. "And you guys be good. I don't want to hear about any fighting when we get home. Understood?"

Katie and John mumbled yes. Tess and I grabbed the wine and dessert and left for the party.

Tess

We were the last ones to get to the party. Jeremy went to hang out with the guys on the patio, and I stayed with the girls in the kitchen. They were getting the food ready.

"There's our pole dancer," Sue said.

Everyone laughed.

At Jeremy's 20th class reunion six months ago, he told everyone at our table I had a pole in our bedroom.

Of course the guys couldn't stop teasing me, even when I explained I didn't use it to strip but to exercise. Apparently, they'd never heard of pole exercise classes.

"You look amazing," Sue said. "Maybe I should get a pole."

"It's not the pole," I explained. "I've been working out at the gym. It keeps me from being bored."

"Honey, if I didn't have to work the last thing I'd be doing is spending the day at the gym," Cookie said.

I took the glass of wine Sue offered me. "I'd rather work."

"Then why don't you?" Sue asked.

"Jeremy doesn't want me to."

Kris sipped her wine. "Why?"

"Where do I start? I think it all boils down to him liking the way things are. I take care of everything at home, and he doesn't have to worry about anything—the kids, the cooking and cleaning and ironing. Everything."

Kris held up her hand. "Let me guess: He doesn't want that to change."

"Precisely. And if I worked, he'd have to help with those things. To be honest, things haven't been good between us."

Sue hugged me. "I'm so sorry you're going through all of this. And as much as I sometimes wish I didn't have to work, it does make me feel good about myself, so I get how you're feeling. Have you told him how upset you are?"

"Who's upset?"

Gina walked into the kitchen. She'd been in the bathroom.

Gina noticed me sitting next to Cookie. "Tess!"

"You look amazing pregnant," I said.

"That's what I told her," Sue said. "When I was pregnant with Chloe my complexion was terrible. I guess it was all the excess oil. But Gina's beautiful."

"Thanks," Gina said. "But I feel like a hippo, and I've pulled out more nipple hairs than I care to count."

Cookie laughed. "I have nipple hairs and I'm not even pregnant. Just be careful when you pull out the nipple hair, you pull it straight out. There's nothing worse than an ingrown nipple hair. Been there, done that."

Gina smiled. "I'll keep that in mind. Now, do you have any advice on how to combat constipation? These prenatal vitamins are doing a number on me."

"It's the iron," Cookie said. "I never knew how much I missed my daily dump until I became pregnant."

Everyone laughed.

"So you had that problem, too?" Gina asked.

"Big time," Cookie said. "I did everything I was told to do—drank lots of water, ate high fiber foods and I walked every day. The doctor switched me to another prenatal vitamin that contained less iron and allowed me to take a stool softener if things got too bad."

"Can we talk about something besides nipple hairs and shit?" Kris asked. "I'd rather talk about sex."

Cookie nodded at me. "Tess isn't having sex."

"Why no sex?" Gina asked.

"She's pissed at Jeremy," Sue said.

"So you were the one who was upset when I walked in. I knew I wasn't hearing things."

Maybe it was the wine making me loosen up, but I knew I was going to lose it when I felt my lip tremble. Seconds later, I melted into a blubbering puddle of tears. "I love my kids. I really do. It's just I want to be more than a mom. Is that so wrong? To need more in my life? I used to be a magazine art director, a damn good one. But Jeremy is so stubborn. But I don't care anymore. I told him to fuck off. I'm getting a job whether he likes it or not."

Jeremy

I grabbed a beer from the cooler and sat down beside Tom. "Thanks for having us over."

"No problem. Sue loves entertaining."

"Sounds like things are going well between you two."

Tom ran his fingers through his hair. "Yeah. I can't believe it. I never thought she'd agree to move in with me. It's great having Chloe here, too. I've never been happier."

"So when are you going to get married?" Keith asked.

Tom pointed to Mike. "He's first."

Mike grabbed another beer and twisted off the cap. "If it were up to me, Gina and I would already be married. Gina wants to wait until after the baby's born. She wants a big church wedding and doesn't want to waddle down the aisle."

I laughed. "Waddle?"

"Her word, not mine. For the record, she doesn't waddle. And I think she's as sexy as hell pregnant."

"Tess was, too," I said. "And the best part of her being pregnant was getting her pregnant. I think we screwed every day every which way. Now, we never do."

Mike cleared his throat. "So things aren't any better between you two?"

"No. In fact, they've grown worse."

"Whoa, I missed this story. Start over from the beginning," Keith said.

I took a sip of my beer. "Tess wants to work. I don't want her to work. She told me to fuck off; she's going to work anyway. And we haven't had sex because we fight all the time."

Cookie's husband, Rick, took a break from the peanut bowl. "So let her work. I'd rather have sex than a clean house. Besides, you can hire someone to cook and clean. You can't hire someone to screw."

I laughed. "Actually, you can."

"You know what I mean," Rick said.

"How about you and Cookie?" I asked. "Are things good?"

"Damn good," Rick said. "She's losing weight; looking good."

I looked at Keith. "And I'm not even going to ask you because I know things are always wild and crazy between you and Kris. I still can't believe you screwed for thirty-one days straight."

Keith cleared his throat. "Actually, it ended up being sixty."

"Damn," I said. "You're one lucky son of a bitch."

Rick took another break from the peanut bowl. "Why'd you stop after sixty?"

"I needed a break," Keith said. "And I bought Kris a vibrator."

"Weren't you worried she'd like the vibrator more than you?" I asked.

"Not really."

"Cookie uses a vibrator, and she still wants the real thing. Actually, we've used both together."

"Oh, Christ," I said. "I need to break out the whiskey I brought."

Tess

"Time to lighten the mood," Cookie said. She pinched her belly fat. "I found a way to get rid of this, and it doesn't require exercise or starving yourself."

Cookie immediately got everyone's attention. Who doesn't want their teen stomach back?

"You stand naked in front of the mirror and put your arms up and reach for the ceiling, and it goes away."

We laughed.

"Cookie, you always make me smile," Kris said. "But you do look like you lost some weight."

Cookie smiled. "Fifteen pounds so far."

"That's awesome," Gina said. "You're losing and I'm gaining."

"Yeah," Cookie said, "but you're gaining for a good reason, unlike me who gained because of my love affair with sweets. Crème-filled donuts? Oh, yeah! Oreo cookies? Couldn't get enough of them. Ice cream? Are you kidding me? Every day!"

"You're just bigger boned," Sue said. "You wouldn't look healthy being super thin."

Sue was right. Cookie always was a little meaty, but she had a beautiful face. And I loved her side swept bangs and the way her blonde hair fell to her shoulders and kind of fanned out. Her pale green eyes always seemed to sparkle.

"Thanks, but I was packing it on. Besides, I want to be thin enough that I don't mind having sex with the lights on or doing it in daytime, both of which Rick enjoys."

"What is it about sex with the lights on that turns guys on?" Sue asked. "I'd rather do it in the dark."

"Me too," Kris said.

Gina rubbed her baby bump. "But letting your partner see you naked is a sign of trust and confidence. Mike sees me naked all the time, and I love the intimacy."

"What about you, Tess?" Cookie asked. "Lights on or off?"

"Well, when we had sex I didn't mind some light. We have a dimmer switch in the bedroom, so that made it easy to control."

"So you weren't kidding about cutting Jeremy off?" Gina asked.

I could feel my face heat up. I blinked back the tears I felt gathering in my eyes. "I just don't feel like having sex with him lately. I've been too pissed. And when I'm pissed, the last thing I want is his penis anywhere near me."

"That's pretty pissed," Sue said.

"Yeah, I'm thinking I need time away from him."

"You're not talking about a separation, are you?" Cookie asked.

I shook my head. "Maybe a little vacation. You know how when you're pissed at someone every little thing they do pisses you off even more?"

"Definitely," Cookie said.

"So, I was thinking that maybe I needed a little alone time. It might do me good just to take a vacation without Jeremy and the kids."

"Hey, maybe we should go on a trip somewhere. Just the girls," Sue said. "That'd be fun. Like to the beach or something."

Gina patted her bump. "Count me out, but the rest of you go, have a great time and come back and tell me all about it."

"Rick and I are going on a cruise to Bermuda," Cookie said. "It'll be the first time we go away without the girls. I haven't bought a bathing suit in forever and was shocked by the prices."

"Tell me about it," Sue said. "I don't understand why bathing suits, and bras for that matter, cost so much when there's hardly anything to them."

We laughed.

Cookie poured another glass of wine. "So I have a dilemma. I have my annual pap smear the day before our cruise. I want to shave my who-ha before we go."

"I think nowadays doctors see more bald vaginas than hairy ones," Kris said. "I know when I started to shave mine, I just told my doctor before she examined me things looked a little different down there. It didn't seem to faze her at all."

"That's because your doctor was female," Cookie said. "I have a male doctor, and I feel weird with him seeing my bald who-ha."

"So shave after your appointment," Gina said.

"That's where the dilemma comes in. If the lab results come back abnormal, which they have in the past, the doctor will want to see me again. I wouldn't be able to see him until after the cruise. And if I shave my who-ha for the cruise, when I go back to the doctor he'll see my once hairy who-ha is now bald."

Gina laughed. "Zip-a-dee-who-ha!"

Gina's comment had everyone in tears from laughing so hard. Cookie's obsession about shaving her who-ha totally cracked me up. The girl was priceless and I knew that conversation would be the highlight of the evening.

"And another thing," Cookie said. "Is it me or are the lips in our southern hemisphere getting thin?"

Kris slapped her leg. "I thought it was only me. Thank god it's not! But yeah. What the hell?"

"It's called getting older," Sue said. "Just as the lips on your face thin with age, so do the ones down south."

"I already made up my mind that if the lips on my face get too thin, I'm getting collagen injections," Kris said. "I hate thin lips."

"I have far bigger problems than thin lips down under," Cookie said. "That whole nether area hasn't been the same since having the twins. Damn! If I could only have the vagina of my youth."

"You can," I said. "Vaginoplasty tightens your vagina to its pre-pregnancy condition. And if you get perineoplasty, that'll take care of the outer looseness."

"Do you just know this stuff or did you get a tuck you haven't told us about?" Sue asked.

"No tuck. Yet. Read about it in a magazine."

"I'll have to look into that," Cookie said. "A tight vagina would be good."

We laughed so hard I'm sure the neighborhood could hear us.

Chapter 4

Jeremy

"Sounds like the girls are having a good time," Tom said. "Ever wonder what they talk about?"

"All the time," Mike said. "I'd love to have one of those invisibility cloaks and listen in."

"Their conversations are probably not nearly as interesting as we think," Keith said.

"I don't know, bro," Rick said. "My guess is any conversation involving my wife has the potential to be X-rated."

I laughed. "True. You do have a point. Cookie's a lot of fun."

Rick rolled his eyes. "That she is. But sometimes she says things you'd rather not know."

"Like what?" Mike asked.

"Believe me, you don't want to know."

Tom got up from his chair. "You guys hungry for some burgers? I'll see if the girls are ready."

Rick polished off the bowl of peanuts on the table. "I thought you'd never ask."

Tom turned on the gas grill and went inside.

"So Jer," Mike said. "I really don't think Tess working will be that bad. It might even make things better at home because she'll feel better about herself. And, when a woman feels good about herself, that's usually better for us."

"Usually?" Rick said. "I'd say it's almost always better for us. A happy woman is a horny woman. Happy wife; happy life."

Keith took a handful of chips from the bowl. "I agree. Besides, helping out around the house is no big deal. So the house might not be as clean as it is now; at the end of the day, who's going to notice—or care?"

"Do you guys ever fight?" I asked.

"Hell yes," Rick said. "But to be honest, I think that's a good thing. At least it is for us. You guys know Cookie. She definitely has a mind of her own. I like that she speaks it and stands up for what she believes in. It might drive me crazy sometimes, but I think it adds a spark to our marriage."

I looked at Mike. "What about you and Gina?"

"Fight? No. Not yet, anyway."

Keith waved his hand. "Hell, they've just gotten back together after 20 years. Of course it's great. Give it time. Kris and I fight, but at the end of the day, I don't want anyone else in my bed."

Tom returned with a plate of burgers.

I pointed to him. "I bet you and Sue don't fight."

"Not really. But I can tell when Sue's getting angry or upset. She'll sigh or roll her eyes or clam up. Anger follows a bell curve, and if I ignore it and it gets to the top of that curve I know it's going to be all downhill from there."

"Sort of like an orgasm," Rick said. "That's one hell of a bell curve."

I laughed. "You're one horny son of a bitch, aren't you?"

Rick shrugged. "Well, I haven't had it all week. Cookie's been PMS-ing and believe me that when she's PMS-ing you don't want to get near her. Between the mood swings and headaches and cramps you'd think she was being tortured."

"And the bloating," Keith said. "Don't forget the bloating. Kris has 'good jeans' and 'I'm bloated' jeans. And when I see her in the 'I'm bloated' jeans I figure it will be a good five days until I get any action. And even then it's iffy."

I laughed. "I figure having your period must feel like you're pissing your pants all day long and that can't be comfortable."

"Who's pissing their pants?" asked Gina as she walked out the door.

I had to practically scream through the laughter. "I was just saying I need to go to the bathroom before I piss my pants. Too much beer."

I headed inside.

Tess

"Quick, while Gina's outside checking on the guys," Sue said. "I bought everything for the baby shower at the party store. You guys are coming early to help decorate, right?"

"I'll be there," I said. "I'm still supposed to pick up the pink balloons, right? Are you sure you don't want me to make tea sandwiches? I just tried a new recipe using ham, brie and apple, and it's delish."

"I can never say no to your tea sandwiches," Sue said. "They're incredible. But are you sure you have the time?"

"Absolutely. I'll bring a tray."

Sue looked at Kris. "And you're bringing the cake, right? And Cookie, you bought the gifts for the games."

Everyone nodded.

"I think we're good to go then."

Gina walked back in. "The guys want to eat outside. Guess we should join them."

"Do we have to?" I asked.

Gina smiled. "Well, it would probably be the nice thing to do."

"As long as I don't have to sit next to my husband," I said. "When he gets drunk he gets obnoxious, and I could tell by the way he looked when he walked in to go to the bathroom he has a buzz on."

"And I'm PMS-ing," Cookie said, "So everything Rick does this week pisses me off. And that includes breathing."

We laughed.

Gina sipped her tea. "I'm lucky. I really don't get bad PMS."

Cookie said what we were all thinking. "You suck! And I bet you can wear your skinny jeans the entire week."

"So true," Kris said. "I have normal clothing and period clothing. And anytime I can wear sweats, I do."

"It's been nice not getting my period," Gina said. "I won't be looking forward to getting that back when I have the baby."

"But at least you won't be constipated," I said.

"True."

Cookie laughed. "Listen to us talking about periods and constipation. We're like a bunch of old women playing bridge bitching about all their health problems."

"Do you think we'll have sex when we're in our 70s?" Kris asked.

"Hell, I'm going to have it as long as I can," Cookie said. "Nowadays with Viagra and other drugs available, there's no reason for a man to be a limp dick."

"Somehow I can't picture me going down on Keith when he's 80," Kris said. "All I can picture is a wrinkled dick curled up like a cat."

"But, like Cookie said, Viagra can turn that cat into a lion."

Jeremy

Tom flipped the burger. "Does anyone want rare?"

"I'll take rare," I said.

Tess scrunched her nose. "I want mine well-done."

"Me too," Gina said. "No pink."

"No pink for me either," Sue said.

It ended up the guys wanted rare or medium rare and the girls wanted well-done. "Is there anything guys and girls agree on?" I asked.

"We agree to disagree," Sue said.

Cookie laughed. "We agree we're mostly right."

"Whoa, whoa, whoa!" Rick said. "You're wrong a lot."

Cookie put her hands on her hips. "When was the last time I was wrong?"

"Last week. At 80s' trivia night."

"Oh, Christ," Cookie said. "Who here knows there was an upscale restaurant above Cheers?"

"I do," I said. "Sam was always fighting with them."

"There was a restaurant above Cheers?" Gina asked.

"That's what I'm talking about," Cookie said.

"So what was it?" Sue asked.

I smiled. "Melville's Fine Sea Food."

"Here's the thing about guys," Cookie said. "You remember stupid shit. Like who in the hell cares if they know the name of the restaurant that was above the Cheers bar in a sitcom that ran 10 years longer than it should have."

"It only ran 11," Rick said.

"My point exactly. It ran 10 longer than it should have. And besides, I bet you don't know the name of Murphy Brown's television show?"

"Who's Murphy Brown?" I asked.

"See?" Cookie said. "You remember a show with a bunch of guys sitting around a bar drinking, but a show with a hard-hitting investigative journalist filled with political satire escapes you. Even Dan Quayle mentioned the show in a campaign speech."

Gina shook her head. "I remember that. It became known as the Murphy Brown speech."

"Now that's a name from the past," I said. "Whatever happened to him?"

Cookie shrugged. "Who knows."

"For the record," Tom asked. "What was the name of Murphy's Brown's show?"

"FYI," Cookie said.

"For Your Improvement," Rick said. "That makes sense."

Cookie shook her head. "You're wrong; For Your Information."

"Okay, smarty pants, what's the name then?" Rick asked.

"For Your Information."

Rick smiled. "I knew that. I was just trying to get you going."

"Sure you were," Cookie said. "Good try but no save."

Tess

Judging by the near empty whiskey bottle sitting in front of Jeremy and his increasingly slurred speech, I knew I'd be the one driving home. I hadn't seen him this drunk in a long time.

Tom's burgers and the food everyone brought to share were delish. I was stuffed and was nursing my wine. We had finished eating a while ago and were sitting around drinking and reminiscing.

"You remember the time we snuck into the pool and went skinny dipping?" Mike asked.

Gina nodded. "Do I ever. I cut my leg climbing over the chain linked fence."

"And I had to help you over because the guys were already buck ass naked in the pool," Cookie said.

Gina took a sip of her hot tea. "We really did have a lot of fun."

"And if my girls turn out to be even half as bad as I was I'll kill them," Cookie said. "I'll never tell them the things I did. Never!"

"Chloe's pretty level headed," Sue said. "But I still worry."

"Is she still dating Rob?" Gina asked.

"He's a good kid," Tom chimed in.

"Yes, he is," Sue said. "But good kids like Chloe and Rob can get into trouble, too."

"Have you talked to her about sex?" Kris asked.

"Absolutely," Sue said. "And I told her more than once when she thinks she's ready for that kind of relationship to let me know, and I'd take her to get birth control. The last thing I want is Chloe to get pregnant."

Kris pushed back her chair. "Be right back. My bladder is about to burst."

A couple of minutes later, Jeremy followed. I could tell by the way he staggered he was drunk.

I pushed out my chair. "I better go check on him. He seems pretty lit."

When I walked into the kitchen I heard Jeremy. "Sixty days straight! That's impressive."

"He told you about that?" Kris asked.

"Yeah. And he also told me about all the fun you had with the chocolate."

I walked through the kitchen and around the corner just in time to see Kris push past Jeremy.

Kris looked at me. "He's wasted. Big time."

Jeremy fell against the wall. "Am not."

I looked at him sprawled out on the floor. "You're a jerk, Jeremy. Find your own ride home."

When I walked back outside, Kris was yelling at Keith. "So you really told everyone about the blindfold and chocolate?"

Keith rubbed his neck. "We were just talking. It was guy talk."

"See if I ever let you find chocolate on me again!" Kris yelled.

I grabbed my purse off the chair. "I'm leaving. And when you see Jeremy, tell him he can walk home!"

Gina and Sue were out of their chairs and running toward me.

"What happened?" Sue yelled.

"Yeah. What went on in there?" Gina asked.

I turned around. "Jeremy is drunk and was being a jerk. Right now, I can't stand to be around him another minute."

As I got in the car I saw Kris getting into her car. It looked like both of us were leaving—and without our husbands.

Chapter 5

Jeremy

I was face down on the hallway floor when I felt hands around my arms.

"Come on, big boy," Mike said. "Let's get you some coffee."

"Jer, you are such a fuckin' dick," Keith said. "I can't believe you said something to Kris about the blindfold and chocolate. I told you not to say anything. Christ. That's the last time I tell you anything!"

I was sitting on a kitchen chair. The room was spinning, and I swayed. "I just told her 60 days straight was impressive."

"Fuck," Keith yelled. "You've got one big mouth!"

Sue walked in from outside carrying my bottle of whiskey. She held it up. "I didn't realize how much Jeremy drank."

"God damn, Jer," Mike said. ""You're not in high school anymore. No wonder you're so drunk."

"Do you think we should go after Kris and Tess?" Gina asked.

Cookie pointed to Keith. "I think Keith should go home and talk to Kris. And I think we should give Tess some space. After what she told us tonight, I think she needs it."

"What'd she tell you?" I asked.

I tried to speak normal, but my words slid out of my mouth like thick syrup and spread, one into the other. "Did she tell you she won't have sex with me? Did she tell you she wants to get a job? Why in the fuck does she want to work? I don't need other guys looking at what I have, trying to take it."

"At the rate you're going, another guy wouldn't have to try too hard," Cookie said. "You're pushing her away all on your own."

"Fuck you, Cookie."

"Double fuck you, Jeremy."

"Come on, Cookie," Rick said. "Let's take Keith home."

"Yeah," Keith said, "because if I stay here any longer, Jeremy's going to have my fist in his face."

"Sue," Gina said. "Feel like sleeping at my house tonight? Who knows how long it's going to take Tom and Mike to sober Jeremy up? And I'm tired."

"Sounds good. I'll grab a bag."

"Thanks, Gina," Tom said.

"Are you going to be all right, babe?" Mike asked. "Sorry about this."

"It's not your fault," Gina said.

Tom sat a cup of coffee in front of Jeremy. "Drink it."

"I was just kidding around with Kris."

"I don't think Kris thought it was funny," Mike said. "You betrayed Keith's trust by sharing something he told you in confidence."

"It's Tess's fault. I'm drinking because she hasn't been putting out."

"Fuck you, Jeremy," Gina said. "Sex isn't something you take. It's something you have with someone you love. Grow up, or you'll lose her for good."

I took a sip of the coffee. "Damn, it's hot. Burned the roof of my mouth."

"I think you burned a lot more than the roof of your mouth tonight," Sue said. "Gina, let's go."

Tess

What a dick! I was so mad at Jeremy I felt like I was going to explode. My anger was thickening like a black storm cloud, and I knew it was only a matter of time before it rained havoc on my life.

As soon as I turned onto the highway, I screamed. I figured no one would hear me and for some reason screaming always makes me feel better. I didn't want to go home just yet. I figured I'd get some coffee and think.

I took the next exit and pulled into a diner. I live on the west side of the city, and I figured there'd be less of a chance I'd run into someone I knew if I went to a diner on the east side. I didn't want to talk to anyone. I just wanted to be alone. I slid into a booth next to a large window. It was almost midnight and the diner was dead, except for a few truckers sitting at the counter nursing coffee.

A middle-age waitress with eyebrows penciled in and a 60s beehive hairdo walked over. "Hey, Hon, what can I get you? Coffee? Sandwich? Pie?"

"Coffee, please."

"That's it? Nothing to eat?"

I shook my head. "Just coffee."

She walked away, and I stared out the window. The diner was on a main road bordered on both sides with stores and restaurants. You could probably find just about anything you wanted to eat on this strip—from Vietnamese and Japanese to American and Mexican.

The waitress returned with my coffee. "Here you go. Cream?"

"Yes, please. Double."

She pulled four creamers out of her maroon apron pocket. "If you need anything else, just holler."

I took a sip of my coffee. It was hot, just like I like it. That's one thing I hate about the club. Its coffee is never hot. You'd think a place that costs thousands of dollars to join and hundreds a month in fees could at least serve you hot coffee. Leave it to the diner and Lucy (that was the name on her pin) to serve the best coffee I had in a long time.

I was trying to figure out what went wrong with me and Jeremy. Was it me? Him? Both of us? Was I being too selfish in wanting to get a job? But he worked, so why couldn't I? I remember what it was like when I worked and had my own money. I didn't feel guilty about buying a new outfit or spending money on something I wanted but didn't need. Jeremy has never denied me anything, but it felt good having my own money and being able to spend it on whatever I liked. I hated relying on him for money.

Most of the woman at the club had no problem with their husbands taking care of them, but I wanted to take care of myself. I wasn't necessarily looking for a full-time job, but just something that would give me a little mad money and make me feel better about myself.

I was swimming in my thoughts when a loud group of kids walked into the diner. They looked to be in their early twenties, and I could tell they'd been drinking.

The waitress led them to the large corner booth and the six of them slid into the large curved seat. Listening to their laughter and banter and watching them be silly took me back to my college years. Jeremy and I along with our friends always ended up in a diner. We'd go to a club and usually about two in the morning we'd roll into a diner for coffee and greasy breakfast.

I couldn't help smiling, remembering those years before life became so complicated. How does that happen? One day you're young and free and loving life and the next you're pushing forty with kids, realizing some of the best years of your life are in the rear-view mirror.

"More coffee, hon?"

I nodded.

"You look like you were deep in thought," the waitress said.

"Yeah. Guess you could say that."

"Man troubles, huh?"

"What?"

"By the look on your face, must be a man's on your mind."

I sighed. "Yeah. Man troubles."

"I was married once. Long time ago. Thank god I dumped him before he dragged me to hell along with him. He was in love with the bottle. Now he's in jail. Too many DUIs."

"Sorry to hear that," I said.

The waitress waved her hand. "I'm not. He deserves to be in jail. Serves him right. He's a loser. But now your man, I bet he's not a loser."

"Not really," I said. "I mean, he's not a drunk, except tonight he had too much to drink and made a total ass out of himself."

She chuckled. "Done that plenty in my life."

"But he's a good provider," I quickly added.

"By the size of the rock on your finger, I figured as much. Unless it's one of those fake ones. Mary Lou, who works the early morning shift, she has a fake one. She thinks we all think it's real, but we don't. Why would she be working here if it was?"

I rubbed my diamond. "It's not fake."

"I knew that. Someone as pretty as you wouldn't have a fake ring. Any more coffee?"

I placed my hand over my cup. "No, thank you. Just the check."

Jeremy

"This coffee tastes like gasoline," I said.

"It's hazelnut," Tom said. "Sorry, it's all I had."

"Shut up and drink it," Mike said.

"Why's everyone pissed at me?"

"I'm pissed because you ruined my night," Mike said. "By now I'd hoped to be rolling in bed with Gina."

"She rolls and she's that pregnant?" I asked.

"It was a figure of speech. Of course she doesn't roll. Forget it. The last thing I want to be doing is talking to you about my sex life."

"I was sort of enjoying the conversation."

"Fuck you, Jer," Mike said. "Just drink the damn coffee."

"You know it's going to take more than coffee," Tom said. "It's going to take time."

I yawned. "I'm tired."

"He's already ruined our night," Tom said. "How about if we just let him sleep it off? We can put him in the guest bedroom."

"You're probably right," Mike said.

Tom ran his fingers through his hair. "You don't have to stay."

"I'm not going anywhere," Mike said. "We're going to have a talk in the morning. Besides, Sue's with Gina, so I might as well sleep here."

"Don't I get a say?" I asked.

"No!" Mike and Tom said.

Next thing I knew I was in a strange bed—alone.

Tess

I found Cassie asleep on the couch and the TV on. I nudged her. "Cassie, I'm home."

She stirred. "What time is it?"

"Almost midnight."

Cassie sat up and sighed. "Did you have fun?"

"It was okay."

"Where's Mr.?"

"I left him there."

"Oh."

I could tell by Cassie's puzzled look she knew something was up, but I wasn't about to go into details with my 17-year-old babysitter. "How were the kids?"

Cassie stood. "Great. We played John's new video game, and Katie and I made rubber band bracelets."

I handed Cassie thirty bucks. "Thanks for watching them."

"Anytime," Cassie said. She held up the bills. "And thanks for this. There's a new shirt I've been dying to get."

I smiled. Oh to be young again, when the most important thing on your mind was buying the revealing shirt at the mall you knew your parents wouldn't approve of—and wearing it under a sweatshirt you'd later remove.

Cassie left and I went to bed—and locked the door.

Chapter 6

Jeremy

Damn. I hadn't felt this messed up in a long time. My hangover had a real attitude. It took me a few minutes to realize I wasn't in my bed. Hell, I wasn't even in my home. I sat up to try and get my bearings, but my head hurt even more when I moved. My throat felt like sandpaper. I needed something to drink and something for the pain. I stumbled downstairs.

"Look who finally decided to get up," said Tom, looking up from reading the morning newspaper.

I held up my hand. "Don't even say it. Just please get me something for this killer headache."

"I have some pills upstairs. Be right back." Tom ran up the steps.

"How about some coffee?" Mike said.

"I think I better stick with water."

Mike filled a glass with water and handed it to me.

I sat down. "So how big of an ass did I make of myself last night?"

"Pretty big," Mike said.

"And Tess?"

"She's pissed, Jer. Really pissed. You really fucked up last night."

Tom returned with the pills. "Here. Take two. You should probably eat something. Taking them without food might upset your stomach."

I shook my head. "Just thinking about eating something makes me want to puke. Maybe a little later. How about laying it on me?"

"You want all of it?" Mike asked.

I nodded. "Might as well find out how deep the shit I'm in is."

"It's pretty deep," Tom said.

Ten minutes later, I had the cliff notes. How I blurted out all of the things Keith had privately shared with me about Kris and his sex life. How Tess and Kris left pissed off. How Keith was so pissed he wanted to slam me a good one.

I buried my head in my hands. "What do I do now?"

"For starters, I think you go see Kris and Keith and apologize," Mike said. "And then you need to work things out with Tess."

I took a gulp of water. "I'm not sure that's possible."

"Maybe you two need some time away—alone," Tom said. "Capture what you lost."

"I'm not sure she'd go. We haven't gone away as a couple since we had kids."

"Sounds like you're due then," Mike said.

"Yeah, at least try," Tom said. "Sometimes you need to look at the past to figure out what to do with the future."

Tess

I was up before the kids, which is unusual on a weekend. But I couldn't sleep. I tossed and turned all night, thinking about Jeremy and what a jerk he was. I couldn't believe our marriage was such a mess.

I remembered our first big fight. He was in dental school, and I was working. We had moved in together, thinking it'd be easier for both of us. It was—for him. But I felt like his maid, not his lover. I was always picking up after him. I did the grocery shopping and laundry and made all of the meals. At first, I didn't mind. In a way, it made me feel "grown-up." But the more I did, the more he came to expect. And then I felt unappreciated. And when he partied the night away with his friends after taking his last final, while I sat at home with a celebration dinner that grew colder by the hour, I'd had enough. That's when the shit really hit the fan, and I moved out.

It didn't take him long to figure out what he'd lost, and I made him work hard to get it back. It occurred to me that life was perhaps repeating itself. I did everything—and I felt unappreciated. But the situation was different. I wasn't his girlfriend; I was his wife and the mother of his children. And leaving him would mean disrupting the lives of our children and that was the last thing I wanted to do. But if I stayed, and nothing changed, I'd be miserable. Unless we could fix our marriage—together.

"Mommy, are you all right?" asked Katie, bouncing into the kitchen.

"I'm fine, sweetie. Why'd you ask?"

Katie shrugged. "Just wondered. With you and Dad fighting and all."

I took a sip of coffee. "Sorry about that. Sometimes parents disagree and argue. Just like kids."

Katie's eyes widened. "But you argue a lot."

"Well, sometimes parents argue a lot."

"You're not getting a divorce, are you?"

"No. Of course not."

"Good, because Angela's parents argued all the time and they got divorced and now she has a bedroom at her mom's house and one at her dad's house."

"Come here." I wrapped my arms around Katie and kissed her on the cheek. "Dad and I will try to work things out. I promise."

Katie pulled away from me so she could look me in the eyes. "Pinky promise?"

"Pinky promise," I said. "We'll try."

"Oh, almost forgot. Grandma called to see if you and John wanted to go to the movies and spend the night."

Katie jumped up and down. "I do! I do!"

John walked in and yawned. "You do what?"

I looked at John. "Grandma wants to take you to see that new movie and said you could sleep over."

John yawned again. "Cool. Definitely. Is she picking us up?"

"I told her I'd drop you off. I'll call her now and let her know it's a go."

Jeremy

Mike offered to take me home.

"Do you mind stopping by Keith's?" I asked.

"Are you sure you want to do that first thing?"

I sighed. "Yeah. I need to apologize."

By the time we arrived at Keith's, it was already early afternoon. I knocked on the door, and I heard his bulldog, Diesel, barking.

Keith opened the door. By the way his lips were mashed together and his eyes narrowed, I could tell he was still steaming.

"Can I come in?"

He stepped aside and waved me in.

"Kris," Keith yelled. "Jer's here."

Kris walked into the living room, twisting a floral kitchen towel in her hands.

"Look guys," I said. "I'm sorry about last night. I had too much to drink. It's no excuse, I know." I looked at Kris. "Sorry for being such a jerk." I took a deep breath and looked down at the floor.

Kris shrugged. "Don't worry about it. I know you were drunk. I was more mad at Keith for telling you about the chocolate hide-and-seek game."

I looked at Keith. "And you have every right to be pissed at me. Go ahead." I stuck out my left cheek. "Take a shot if it'd make you feel better."

Keith waved his hand. "I've had nights where I drank too much too. But damn, Jer. What we talk about has to stay between us."

Kris cleared her throat. "But, like we talked about, there are certain things that are off limits when it comes to discussions with your friends."

"Look, guys," I said, "I totally understand. I just hope you both give me a second chance. It's no excuse, I know. But what's been going on between me and Tess has me more messed up than I realized."

"Then go home and fix it," Kris said. "And if you want my advice, listen to your wife. Really listen. I think if you listen you'll hear more than what's being said."

When I returned to Mike's car, he was on the phone with Gina. "I'll be home soon. We're leaving Keith's now. Love you. Bye."

Mike looked at me. "How'd it go?"

"Better than I thought. They were both pretty understanding, considering. I think Kris was more pissed at Keith than she was at me."

Mike nodded. "Well, then. The next one on your list is Tess."

I shook my head. "And that's definitely not going to be as easy as this was."

"You know what they say," Mike said. "Anything worth having usually isn't easy."

"So Lisa wasn't worth having?" I asked about his ex-wife.

"Things were different with Lisa," Mike said. "Lisa and I were great friends. I thought that was enough. But it wasn't. Lisa deserved more. She deserved to be loved like her husband loves her now. I just wasn't the man for her. My heart always belonged to Gina. It was Lisa who helped me see that. But you, man. When Tess came into your life she turned it upside down. I never saw a woman, and you've had plenty, that had that kind of effect on you."

I licked my lips. "You're right. I thought I was going to marry Betsy. Remember her?"

A smile inched onto Mike's face. "Do I ever. She was one hot chick."

"True. She was. But she was more body than brains, which was fine when I was a freshman."

"What ever happened to her anyway?"

"It was weird," I said. "She just vanished. We broke up at the end of the school year, and she never came back to college. I guess she transferred to another school. I never really found out. But it wasn't long after that I met Tess. And that's when I realized what real love was. I just don't know how I let things get so out of control."

By the time I got home, Tess and the kids were gone. There was a note on the kitchen table saying she was dropping the kids off at my parents'. I jumped in the shower. I couldn't remember the last time Tess and I had taken a shower together. Damn I miss those times.

Tess

I hugged John and Katie. "Be good for Grandma."

"They're always angels," Diana said.

Too bad their father isn't.

"When do you want me to pick them up tomorrow?"

"How about dinner? You and Jeremy come to dinner. I haven't seen my son for a while anyway."

Katie's eyes darted to me.

I winked at Katie. "Dinner sounds great. See you around five then."

On the drive home, I wondered if Jeremy would be there. I really didn't want to face him, but I knew I had to. And, with the kids not around, I had the perfect opportunity.

It occurred to me wanting to go back to work was just part of the problem. If I were honest with myself, we'd been growing a part for a while. I realized we really didn't have a lot of common interests. I had artistic interests. I enjoyed going to concerts and art museums and reading books. Jeremy was more outdoorsy. Given the choice between attending a concert or hiking, he'd choose hiking in the time it took him to smile. Over the years, I accepted his reluctance to attend concerts and do the other things I wanted to do. And instead of not going by myself, or with a girlfriend, I gave in and did the things he wanted to do. I realized I was resentful and mad at myself for giving in and mad at Jeremy for not wanting to do things that made me happy. How do you fix stuff like this? How do you fix something when the other person doesn't think it needs fixing?

I was stopped at a red light near the entrance to the park. I glanced over and saw a young couple sitting on the bench. They faced each other and appeared to be in deep conversation. It reminded me of the first time Jeremy and I said the L word.

It had been a crisp December day and feathery snowflakes floated toward us as we sat on a bench outside Old Main. It was the week before finals and we weren't going to see each other over Christmas break. He was spending his break in Florida with his grandparents, and I was going home hoping to pick up some hours at the department store where I'd worked the previous summer.

We were trying to catch snowflakes on our tongues and I laughed so hard I fell off the bench. Jeremy took my hand and pulled me up and we kissed.

"I have something I want to tell you," I said. "But I'm not sure I should."

His dark eyes swallowed mine. "Just tell me."

"I... I think I love you."

Jeremy picked me off the ground and twirled me around and found my lips. "I love you, too, Tess. But I was afraid of saying it. I didn't want to chase you away. I never felt about a girl the way I feel about you."

That moment, with the snow falling, was one of the happiest moments of my life. Before Jeremy left for break he stopped by my dorm room to give me a present. It was a snow globe.

"Just shake it when you want to remember I love you."

The light turned green. I was lost in my thoughts when the driver behind me laid on his horn. I wondered where that snow globe was. I hadn't seen it in years. Maybe it had been tossed out. Or broken.

Chapter 7

Jeremy

I was watching football when I heard the garage door open. I took a deep breath. Tess was home. I turned off the TV and went to wait for her in the kitchen.

She walked in the door and saw me standing by the counter. "We need to talk. And you need to listen."

I nodded. "I'm sorry about last night. Guess I drank more than I thought."

"Did you apologize to Kris and Keith?"

"I stopped by their house on the way home."

"And?"

"And Kris seemed more pissed at Keith for sharing such personal information."

"I can't blame her," Tess said.

I followed Tess into the family room. She sat on the leather couch, and I sat on the recliner across from her.

"What's happening with us, Tess? I'm not happy. You're not happy. I feel like we've become more like roommates than lovers. Even when we have sex—and it's been a while—it's feels like you're doing me a favor and really not into it."

Tess wrung her hands. "I guess I'm not. I've been so angry at you for not understanding me."

I inched forward on the recliner. "I said you could get a job if that's what you really wanted to do."

Tess got louder and there was a definite sharpness in her tone. "I don't need your permission to get a job or do anything else for that matter. What I want and need is your support."

"Okay. Then I support you."

Tess sighed. "But do you support me because you want to get laid or do you support me because you understand how I feel?"

"Getting laid isn't a bad reason," I said, hoping to get her to loosen up a bit.

"Well, at least you're being honest."

"Look, Tess. I can't pretend. I want to be supportive. Do I understand how you feel? Why you want to work outside the home? No, I don't. I'm sorry. I just don't understand that. But if that's what you want, if it will make you happy, I'm willing to be supportive and do whatever it is I need to do. I don't want to lose you."

"It's not going to be easy," Tess said. "There'll have to be changes. If I work, it means you need to help out with things at home."

"Or we find someone to help you," I said. "Like a cleaning lady. What type of work do you want to do anyway?"

Tess

The fact Jeremy was asking me about the type of work I was looking for threw me a bit. The truth was I wasn't exactly sure. All I knew is I needed to do something for me. I wasn't necessarily looking for a full-time job. I wasn't opposed to it either. I wanted to see what was out there.

"I'm not a hundred percent sure. For starters, I might start teaching cycle classes at the gym. I've looked into the certification process, and I think I could do it."

Jeremy nodded. "That's like a few hours a week, right?"

"I'd probably start teaching three classes a week. So yeah, about three hours. And Yorktown Press is also looking for an art director for its new glossy women's magazine. They haven't formally advertised, but Sue told me about it. Chloe takes gymnastics with the owner's daughter. I might check into that."

"That sounds promising."

"Yeah, we'll see."

I couldn't believe how normal our conversation was. I'd expected it to be peppered with verbal jabs, a few chosen curse words and maybe even a thrown thing or two. But it was reasonably lame in those regards, and I felt myself melting as I caught glimpses of the man I'd fallen in love with. Still, I wasn't ready to sleep with him. I didn't want to feel like he was giving in just so he could get something even if that wasn't the case. And I instinctively knew he'd wait for me to make the first move. Even if he wanted it, he'd wait for me to lead the way. And I was determined to hold out to see if he kept his end of the bargain.

"Are you hungry?"

Jeremy smiled. "Very. Have something in mind?"

"Remember that place we used to go to when we were just starting out?"

"You mean the dump with the cheap hamburgers and skinny fries?"

I nodded. "It might have been a dump, but it did have the best fries. And the hamburgers were made in some kind of sauce."

"I think it's still open," Jeremy said.

"Can we go there?"

"Whatever you want," said Jeremy, standing up. He opened his arms. "Can I hug you?"

I walked over to him and he wrapped his arms around me and I buried my head into his chest.

He kissed the top of my head. "I'm really going to try, Tess. I promise."

Jeremy

Tess and I sat in the corner booth we used to sit in back in the day. "This place hasn't changed much," I said.

Tess rolled her eyes. "I don't think it's changed at all." She looked down at the seat. "The cigarette burn mark is still there."

"You remember the burn mark?"

She nodded. "Yeah. If you look to the right, you'll probably see a tear in the vinyl seat that's been patched with silver duct tape."

I looked and shook my head. "Damn. You're right. And by the look of the duct tape, it's been there for a while."

Tess took a bite of a fry. "But the burgers are still good, and the fries are just the way I like them. Crispy and a little brown."

We ate, reminiscing about all of the things we did when we were young and beginning our life as a married couple. It was easy conversation, like falling into my recliner to watch a football game.

"Remember how Thursdays was Hamburger Helper night?" Tess asked.

I laughed. "Yeah, Hamburger Helper—without the hamburger."

"And Tuesday night was Ramen noodle night," Tess continued. "Beef flavored for you; chicken for me."

I sighed. "It's been a long time since I've eaten Hamburger Helper without the hamburger and Ramen noodles. Maybe we should try it some night. For old times' sake."

The bell on the door jingled. I looked up and waved. "It's Chloe and she's with a guy."

Tess turned around and waved.

Chloe walked over. "Hi, guys! This is Rob. Rob, this is Tess and Jeremy. Jeremy went to high school with my mom and Tom."

Rob held out his hand, and Tess and I shook it.

"Nice to meet you, Rob," Tess said.

He smiled. "Thank you, ma'am."

"Well, we're going to order. It was nice seeing you guys," Chloe said.

"I guess I'll see you next week at Gina's baby shower," Tess said.

Chloe sighed. "Unfortunately I'm going to miss it. My dad's taking me to New York for the weekend. He purchased show tickets and planned the weekend before Mom told me about the shower."

"Ah, too bad. But I'm sure Gina will understand."

They walked away.

"I can't believe Chloe's dating," I said. "Seems like only yesterday she was dragging her doll everywhere she went."

"Kids do grow up," Tess said. "Just look at Katie and John."

I held up my hand. "Don't remind me. It makes me feel old."

Tess

When we got home from the burger joint, Jeremy and I watched a movie. Even though he prefers action and adventure, he agreed to watch a romance. I sat next to him on the sofa, and he put his arm around me but that's as far as it went. I knew he was horny as hell, but I was determined to hold out. I didn't want to have sex too soon and then he'd think everything was fine and go back to his old ways.

"Stupid ass," I said.

Jeremy jumped. "Who you calling a stupid ass?"

I pointed to the TV. "Him. I can't believe he just doesn't tell her how he feels. He loves her. It's obvious. But he won't tell her he loves her because he thinks she loves his best friend."

"She doesn't, though, right?"

"Right. She loves him."

"So they both love each other but neither one is admitting it."

"Precisely," I said.

"So how's this going to end if no one acts?"

I took another sip of wine. "Guess we'll just have to see."

Chapter 8

Jeremy

I was a little nervous about going over to Tom's. He'd invited the guys over to watch football while the girls went to Gina's surprise baby shower. It'd be the first time seeing Keith since I apologized for being drunk and making a complete ass out of myself.

I sipped a beer, waiting for Mike to pick me up. The kids were with my parents, who took them to Washington for the weekend. It wasn't a bad week as far as weeks went. Still no sex, but I felt as if things were improving between Tess and me. I got up with the kids one morning and let her sleep in. I even packed Katie's lunch, although she complained the whole time, telling me "Mom does it better." Hell, I even tried doing a load of laundry, but put too much detergent in the washing machine. Tess ended up having to run the load through the rinse cycle again. I was trying, though, really trying.

Most of the week, I slept in a separate bed. But by mid-week, Tess invited me to sleep with her. She was still holding out, but I could feel she was warming up.

Mike pulled into the driveway and tooted the horn. I grabbed the dessert Tess made for me to take and went outside.

"What's that?" Mike asked as I climbed in.

"Chocolate cake. Tess made it."

Mike licked his lips. "I love Tess's cakes." Mike shook his head. "I didn't mean that how it sounded."

"No problem. I love them, too. Just haven't had them lately."

Mike backed out of the driveway. "So things still haven't improved?"

"A little. But we're still not having sex."

He turned the wheel. "Man, she must've been pissed."

"I hope that's all it is."

He straightened the car and took off. "Do you think there's someone else?"

"Based on how Tess feels about cheaters, I can't imagine that ever happening. Still, I'd be lying if I said the thought hasn't crossed my mind, especially with how shitty everything's been lately. She was offered a job teaching a cycling class at the gym."

"That's great," Mike said.

"Yeah. But I'm beginning to wonder if there isn't someone at the gym."

"Why?"

"Oh, I don't know. Maybe I'm just crazy or paranoid. For example. The other day, Tess told me she was going to the gym. It seemed like she spent forever getting ready. Normally she just throws on sweats and a T-shirt and puts her hair in a ponytail. Instead, she walked downstairs dressed for the gym but wearing makeup, like she was going out on the town. Who wears makeup to the gym?"

"Maybe it just makes her feel better," Mike said.

"Maybe. Or maybe there's someone there she's trying to impress."

"Did you ask her about it?"

"No. I didn't want to piss her off. I'm waiting for her to make the first move. I've been trying to help out more around the house and show her I'm not just talk. But I'm having a tough time breaking through. She was thinking about applying for a full-time job at a new magazine that's starting up."

"Would she still teach cycling classes?"

"Not sure. Guess it would depend on the magazine hours."

Mike pulled up to Tom's house. "Remember, you're moving on. I'm sure Keith wants to put everything behind him just like you do."

I opened the car door. "Let's hope we can."

Tess

Gina followed me down the hall to the room I'd reserved at the country club. She thought she was going to have lunch with Sue and me. I'd dropped off the tea sandwiches earlier before picking Gina up. I opened the door.

"Surprise!"

We walked into a sea of yellows and pinks and blues and mint greens. Because she and Mike opted to not find out the sex of their baby ahead of time, the party palette covered both.

Gina placed her hand over her heart. Her lip trembled, and her eyes turned glassy. She scanned the room, packed with friends and family. "I don't know what to say." She started crying. "I wish Mom were here."

Sue hugged Gina. "She's here. You just can't see her."

That only made Gina cry more. I don't think there was a dry eye in the room.

"Come on," Sue said. "Let's get this party started."

Gina smiled and nodded. Sue led her to the guest of honor chair, decorated with pink and blue steamers and balloons.

"The decorations are adorable," Gina said.

Baby bottles filled with miniature pink and blue carnations decorated each table, along with wooden alphabet blocks and plastic rattles. Guests had hung baby items on a clothes line strung across the room. There were sleepers and undershirts and bibs and other items, mostly in green and yellow. A table overflowed with gifts. Gina had generous friends.

We played games, ate and then Gina opened the gifts. We had a great time and eventually it was just the girls; all of the other guests had left.

"You guys really surprised me," Gina said. "Thank you. This was the best shower ever."

"You've waited a long time to be a mother," Sue said. "We wanted it to be perfect for you."

"It's more than perfect."

"Not to change the subject," Cookie said. "But how's the shitting going?"

Gina laughed. "Better."

"Oh. My. God," Sue said. "Speaking of shitting, did you see that commercial for poop spray on television? It totally cracks me up."

"Poop spray?" Gina asked.

"You spray it in the toilet before you go, and it covers up the odor," Sue explained. "I guess it's to use when you go in a public restroom."

"There's no way I'd ever poop in a public restroom," Gina said.

I agreed.

"Sometimes you don't have a choice," Lynn said.

"True," Cookie said. "And sometimes there's a poop stalemate."

I laughed, waiting for Cookie to explain.

"A what?" Lynn asked.

"A poop stalemate. It's when you go into a public restroom to poop. Someone comes in and you act dead silent, hoping they'll leave quickly. But they don't. They have to poop, too. So you end up in a stalemate. Sometimes you make noise. Like open and shut the tampon trash receptacle attached to the wall or crumple some toilet paper, in an attempt to disguise your true purpose. But it doesn't work. Nobody wins a poop stalemate."

Everyone laughed. I loved hanging out with the girls. They always made me laugh, and I really needed laughter in my life.

Jeremy

When I walked into Tom's house, Keith was drinking a beer at the bar. I walked over and extended my hand. "Sorry again for acting like an asshole."

Keith waved. "Movin' on, Jer."

"What can I get you to drink?" Tom asked.

"Nothing stronger than beer."

Tom handed me a beer, and I sat on the bar stool next to Keith.

Mike opted for beer, too.

"So, Mike, ready for that new baby?"

Mike smiled. "Can't wait."

"Man. Dude. You're telling me you can't wait to be up half the night?" Keith asked.

"Well, I'm not too anxious for that, but I'm damn anxious to hold mine and Gina's baby."

"You are one sentimental dude," Keith joked.

Mike nodded. "When it comes to Gina, you're right. I am. But god, I never in a million years thought we'd be having a baby together. The way it all happened is pretty incredible. And to think I almost didn't go to our reunion."

"Speaking of the reunion," I said, "I ran into Eric the other week. He was home visiting his parents. I guess the Rhode Island school where he teaches had a long weekend."

"How's he doing?" Tom asked.

"About the same. Still doing that Civil War re-enactor thing."

"Remember how he could lure Mrs. Hoffman into spending the entire class telling stories from her childhood?" Mike asked.

We laughed.

"Who could forget Hoffman and her stories?" Tom said. "It beat reading the Iliad."

"Do you think the girls surprised Gina with the shower or was she expecting it?" Rick asked Mike.

"I think she thought they'd have a shower for her, but I don't think she thought it was today. She honestly thought she was having lunch with Sue and Tess at the club."

Tom looked at his watch. "Better turn on the TV. Game's about to start."

Tess

"So are things any better between you and Jeremy?" Gina asked.

"Well, we still aren't having sex, but I've allowed him back in the bed."

"Man, woman, you've got will power," Cookie said. "The last time Rick and I had a fight I could only hold out for a couple of days. Well, the fact that my vibrator went dead, and I didn't have any batteries in the house might've had something to do with it."

"I'm just not going to let him off easy," I said. "I really want him to change."

"Change is tough," Gina said. "Especially for someone like Jeremy who's used to having things his way."

"That's the problem," I said.

"But no partner is perfect," Sue said. "Even Tom's not perfect."

"Agreed," Gina said. "They're still human. Mike, for example, never replaces the toilet paper roll. And somehow I always get stuck on the toilet with the last square clinging to the empty roll."

We laughed.

"Real change takes effort," Sue said. "I think a person has to be committed to changing himself because it's tough to do it for someone else."

"Tell me about it," Cookie said. "I tried and it didn't work."

"What'd you do?" I asked.

"Tried harder not to sweat the small stuff. Like Rick's annoying habit of leaving the damn bath towel on the floor. Every time I pick up after the slob I try to picture the loving things he does for me."

"Does it work?" I asked.

"Honestly? Some of the time. I'd be lying if I said it works all of the time. If I'm PMS-ing, it definitely doesn't work. Then I get pissed off at him if he even looks at me a little wrong."

"Not to change the subject," Gina said, "but I'm worried about sex after the baby. Will it be as good as it was before?"

"My advice? Do kegels," Cookie said. "Trust me, you'll thank me later."

Sue nodded. "Agree. Kegel like crazy."

"Really?"

"Yes, really," Cookie said. "I didn't do them and after I had the twins I couldn't sneeze without pissing a drop. Same thing if I laughed or coughed. It was embarrassing. I smelled like piss. I had to wear pads and it sucked big time. Kegels helped."

Lynn touched her heart with her hand. "I've never been pregnant and do kegels. It makes my orgasms more intense."

"Seriously?" Gina asked.

Lynn smiled. "Absolutely. I do kegels all of the time. In meetings at work, while I'm driving, if I'm out to dinner with friends. If you're talking to me and I'm sitting, I'm probably kegeling."

"Are you doing them now?" Gina asked.

"I was earlier."

"And you know they aren't just for women," Cookie said. "I got Rick to do them. Now he's a regular kegeler. And believe me, he needed the exercises. My nickname for him was Minute Man because that's about how long he'd last. He'd come while I was just getting started. It really used to piss me off. Now, he has more control. And it's improved his climaxes."

"I feel like a beached whale when we have sex," Gina said. "I love being pregnant, but I do wonder sometimes if my stomach will ever be flat again."

"You'll have to come to the gym with me," I said. "I'm thinking about teaching cycling classes."

"Oh, Lord," Cookie said. "There's no way my big ass could fit on one of those tiny cycle seats. I swear they make those things for baby dolls."

"I took a class once," Lynn said, "and my pelvic floor hurt like hell afterward."

"A padded cycle seat and padded shorts can help with that," I said.

Lynn shook her head. "If I'm going to pound something it damn well isn't going to be a cycle seat. I swear I bruised my labia and clitoris on that damn bike. I ended up putting an ice pack on it."

We laughed.

"Besides teaching cycling, are you thinking about any other jobs?" Gina asked.

I wanted to tell them about my idea, but the timing wasn't right. I still had some research to do.

"I'm definitely looking for a job," I said. "I'll only teach three cycle classes a week, and I hope to be able to continue teaching if I get a new job. So we'll see."

Chapter 9

Jeremy

Keith held out his hand. "Pay up."

I dug a twenty out of my pocket and handed it to him. I lost another game bet.

"Hey, you guys interested in getting a poker game together?" Keith asked.

"Sure," I said. "But where?"

"Can't be at my house," Keith said. "Too many kids."

"Why'd you have five anyway?" Mike asked.

"Well, after two sets of twin girls, I was sure the next one would be a boy. And I really wanted a son."

I laughed. "It's good you got him or you'd still be trying."

"We can have the game here," Tom said. "But I'll have to check with Sue first."

"Listen to you, lover boy," I said. "Already running everything by Sue."

Tom shrugged. "I don't think she'll mind, but she lives here, too, so I just think I should ask. Might be better to do it on a weekend Chloe's with her dad."

"Speaking of Chloe, did you see her dad's latest?" Mike asked. "I ran into them at the liquor store."

"Sue's met her; I haven't," Tom said. "But I heard all about The Great Cleavage Catastrophe."

"What's wrong with her cleavage?" I asked.

"I thought it was sort of nice," Mike said.

"According to Sue," Tom explained, "it's better to have a, quote, 'gentle valley,' unquote. Sue says only one or two inches should be visible."

"There was definitely more than two inches visible on that woman," Mike said.

"Yes, Sue told me she had butt-crack cleavage."

We laughed.

"You have to explain that," I said.

"According to Sue, when a woman's breasts are pushed way up and more than three inches is exposed and the breasts are touching, it's butt-crack cleavage. And Sue says butt-crack cleavage is, quote, 'so yesterday,' unquote."

"Well, that's one butt crack I'd like to be between," Rick said.

"Better hadn't ever let Cookie hear you talk like that," Mike said. "She's not someone I'd want to get on the bad side of."

"You're right about that," Rick said. "I made the mistake of telling her what this woman said the other night to me in Joe's Bar. I started playing racquet ball with some guys from work once a week. After the game, we stopped at Joe's. And this woman, who looked a little rough, comes up and asks me if I want some pussy. Just like that. Out of the blue. The broad asks me if I want some pussy. Christ, I spit the swig of beer I'd just taken all over the counter. Her girlfriend was behind her, and they started laughing. Then she shows me this Pussy Energy drink. It was in a white can."

"So it's a real thing?" Tom asked.

"Oh yeah," Rick said. "I think it comes from London. The girls were getting their kicks asking guys if they wanted some pussy. Then they'd whip out the empty can. I thought it was funny and told Cookie about it. Even googled it so she could see it was a real thing. But she wasn't amused."

"Uh-oh," Mike said.

"Uh-oh is right. I didn't get pussy for a couple of nights!"

Tess

We pulled our cars up to the door to load Gina's gifts.

"Just sit and let us do the work," Sue told her.

"I'm not an invalid," Gina said. "I can carry a gift bag or two."

Sue shook her head. "You never listen, do you?"

Gina held up her finger. "Not true. Sometimes I do."

"I can count the number of times on one hand," Sue said.

We loaded the gifts into my car and into Kris's and Lynn's cars. We didn't need Cookie's car, but she followed us to Gina's house to help unload.

Sue road with Cookie and Gina road with me.

"Are you anxious to find out what you're having?" I asked Gina on the ride to her house.

Gina placed her hand on her belly. "Definitely."

"Do you picture the baby being a certain sex?"

"Actually, I picture it being a girl sometimes, and other times I picture it being a boy."

"And you've never been tempted to open the envelope the technician gave you and look at the sex?"

"Oh, I've been tempted. Very tempted. I even went so far as to pick around the edges of the seal. But then I think of Mike and I finding out together. And no matter what the sex is, this baby will be a dream come true—for both of us."

"Are you scared?"

"Terrified is more like it," Gina said. "What if I'm not mommy material? What if I suck at it?"

I reached over and patted Gina's arm. "Oh, Gina, you won't suck at it. I had the same doubts and fears when I was pregnant with John. Just follow your instincts."

"Did you swell?" Gina asked.

"Big time. Hands, feet, face, boobs. My body was one big blob. Everything on me swelled. Even my girl parts."

Gina laughed. "No one ever talks about the girl parts swelling. I couldn't see past my belly, and I held a mirror down there one day. Actually, it was hurting when I sat so I checked it out. I about died when I saw how swollen my labia was. No wonder it hurt so much."

I laughed. "I remember those days. Laying down takes the pressure off, but when you sit or stand, it hurts."

"Yeah, and then if you can manage to have sex, even more blood rushes to that area."

"Tell me about it."

"Have you ever gotten stuck in the toilet?" Gina asked.

I shook my head. "What?"

"Well, the other night I had to go to the bathroom. I didn't turn on the lights. I sat down to pee, and Mike hadn't put the toilet seat down. My ass hit the water, and I became wedged in the toilet and couldn't get out."

I burst out laughing. "Oh, Gina. That's so funny."

"It is now, but believe me it wasn't at the time. I was so pissed at Mike. I yelled for him and when he finally walked into the bathroom and turned on the light and saw me stuck in the toilet he started laughing. And he laughed so hard he was bent over and holding his gut, which made me even madder. I told him to get me the hell out of the toilet, and he pulled me out but he laughed the entire time."

I smiled. "Well, I definitely sat on the toilet not realizing the seat wasn't down, but I never got stuck in it. That's too funny. I bet Mike made sure the toilet seat was down after that."

Jeremy

We hung around after the game for a bit, shooting some pool in Tom's man cave. He had by far the best hangout of any of my friends. Then again, he doesn't have kids who claim every inch of the house.

Besides the usual stocked bar, pool table, oversized recliner chairs and flat screen, Tom had an extensive collection of sport memorabilia.

I looked at Tom's guitars propped in the corner. "Do you still play?"

"Some. Not as much as I used to. I started teaching Chloe, but we haven't gotten too far."

"Remember our band?" Mike asked. "How old were we anyway?

"It was the summer after seventh grade," Tom said, "and we were convinced we'd hit the big time one day."

We laughed.

I pointed to Mike. "Remember how your nosey neighbors called the cops and complained about the noise?"

"I remember. Cops showed up and banged on the garage door. We were practicing and didn't hear them at first. That pissed them off even more."

"They were dicks," I said. "And so were your neighbors. We were just a bunch of kids trying to have some fun. We could've been smoking weed or doing something far worse than trying to make music."

"Well, we did smoke weed," Keith said.

I waved my hand. "Yeah, but that came later. In high school. We're talking seventh grade here."

"And it's not like we were stoners," Tom said. "We mostly drank."

"Seeing the stoners at the class reunion was fun," Mike said. "Remember Bob? He reeked of weed every day in school. I never cared much for him, but Gina always liked him. He was in her homeroom."

"You're talking about Bob Myers," Tom said. "Actually, he's done quite well for himself. Owns a garage, which he recently expanded. He was never one for books, but man could he fix a car like nobody's business."

"Speaking of high school, guess what came on TV the other night?" Keith asked.

We all shrugged.

"Indiana Jones and the Temple of Doom."

Everyone laughed.

"That's one night I'll never forget," I said. "You got totally wasted and threw up all over the lady sitting in front of you."

Keith cleared his throat. "Yeah, but you were the one who smuggled the bottle of vodka into the theater and passed it around."

"I didn't force you to drink it," I said.

"Like I was going to be the only one who didn't take a swig when it came to me. Come on now, I was too cool for that."

We laughed. I don't think any of us would be cool enough to do that today," Mike said.

Tom reached under the bar and grabbed a bottle of vodka and held it up. "Anyone want to try?"

I shook my head, "No way. I'm sticking with beer. It'll keep me out of trouble."

Tess

"Do you think you and Jeremy are going to be all right?" Gina asked.

I sighed. "Honestly, I don't know. I've been doing a lot of thinking these past couple of months. Teaching cycle class would be fun, but I have something bigger in mind. I don't want to share just yet, though."

"What are you up to, Tess?"

"Don't worry. Nothing bad. You'd approve. I just don't want to jinx anything by sharing too soon. And I don't want to give Jeremy the chance to talk me out of it."

"Will he approve?" Gina asked.

"That's the part I'm unsure of. He might think it's a silly idea. That's why I need to do my homework and get everything figured out before I share it with him."

"Oh, so you are going to share it?"

"Yes. Of course. At some point. But not just yet. In the meantime, I'll start the certification process to teach cycle classes. Exercising always helps me work through ideas—and helps me deal with the stress."

"After I have the baby, I'll definitely get a gym membership."

"How much time are you taking off work?"

"Not as long as I'd like: A couple of months. With just starting my practice, I've been extremely busy. Thank God Sue is managing the office for me."

"Do you like what you're doing now? General practice is so different from your prosecution work."

"Yes. More than I thought I would. Don't get me wrong, I loved prosecuting sex crimes, but opening my own practice has always been in the back of my mind. And, who knows, I might even run for judge someday."

"I'd vote for you."

Gina laughed. "Thanks. I still pinch myself sometimes to make sure it's all real. My life has changed so much over this past year. I never in a million years thought I'd be having Mike's baby and we'd be together. It's all I've ever wanted. All I ever dreamed of. But I thought dreams were for other people, not me."

"I'm a firm believer things happen for a reason," I said. "We don't always see the why of something, but eventually it becomes known."

"Mom believed that, too. She'd always say this or that happened for a reason. And then, of course, I'd ask why bad things happen to good people. Was there a reason for that? I was such a smart ass. God, I miss her."

"I can't say I have the answer to that," I told her. "But I do believe in karma, and I've seen it come back to bite some people in the ass."

I pulled into Gina's driveway. "Looks like we're here."

Gina smiled. "It was a beautiful shower, Tess. Thanks so much for helping out."

"Of course. And, uh, Gina?"

Gina tilted her head. "What?"

"You like tea, don't you?"

"Love it. Why?"

I shrugged. "Just wondered. I like tea, too."

Chapter 10

Jeremy

When I returned home from Tom's, Tess was using the laptop at the kitchen table.

"How'd the shower go?" I asked.

She typed while she talked. "Great. Gina was really surprised. How was the game?"

"Tess, can you please look at me? You know I hate when you don't look at me when I'm talking to you."

Tess sat back and put her hands on her lap. "This better?"

"What are you working on anyway?"

She closed her laptop lid. "Nothing important. Just surfing the net. So the game: How was it?"

I pulled out a chair and sat across from her. "Game was good. I do have a bad case of man cave envy."

Tess smiled. "Tom does have a nice hangout."

"I'd say it's more than nice. Makes me want to put on that addition we talked about."

Tess squirmed. "Do you think now's a good time to add a family room?"

I shrugged. "Is anytime good? My practice is doing well. It's as good a time as any. Besides, if we wait too long we'll have college tuition to worry about."

Tess sighed.

"What are you thinking?" I asked.

"I'm just thinking now's not the right time. There are things I want to do."

"What does you finding a job have to do with us putting on an addition?"

"For one, I won't be here during the day."

"So we make sure we find a reputable builder. There's a home show at the expo center this weekend. I was thinking we could go tomorrow. Walk around and talk to some builders. Maybe even get some ideas."

"Okay. But just because I'm agreeing to go doesn't mean I'm agreeing to building the addition."

"I thought you'd be excited about this."

"Well, I might have some other plans."

"What in the hell is that supposed to mean, Tess? What other plans?"

Tess put her finger to her lips. "Shh! The kids have friends over, and I don't want them to hear us fighting."

I stood and shook my head. "I really don't get you, Tess. I'm trying, but you're sure making it difficult."

Tess

Normally, I'd have been ecstatic about adding a family room. Jeremy and I have talked about it ever since we bought the house from his parents. But I was working on a plan that would cost money, and I knew building the addition might mean kissing my plan goodbye. Jeremy's man cave envy meant figuring out things in a hurry.

I had an important meeting on Monday, and I was trying to finish my research. I wasn't ready to share my plan with Jeremy or anyone else quite yet. I still had a long way to go before I knew if it was even feasible.

Katie walked into the kitchen. "I'm bored."

"I thought Angie was here."

"She had to go home."

"Go play with your brother."

Katie put her hands on her hips. "Really, Mom. There's no way I want to hang out with fart face."

"Who you calling fart face?" John walked into the room.

"Wouldn't you like to know," Katie said.

"Booger brain," John said.

"Butt face," Katie flung back.

"Nerd turd!"

"Poopy pants!"

I stood. "Enough. Stop it. How am I supposed to work with you two fighting all the time?"

"You and Dad do it," Katie said.

I sighed. "You know what? I really need to get some work done. Both of you: go to your rooms until you can figure out how to be nice to one another."

"Not fair. She's the one who started it," John said.

"Now! To your rooms. Both of you!"

Katie and John stumped away. I heard them mutter something, but I couldn't make it out. I wondered if they'd ever like each other.

I returned to my work, but the more I dug into it the more confused I became. Meeting with my mentor again would help. I had some ideas, and I was anxious to share them with him. I considered confiding in Gina on the way to her house after the shower, but decided against it. She had enough on her mind, and I didn't want to burden her with my problems or keeping any secrets from Mike. And since Mike is Jeremy's best friend, I definitely didn't want him to know what I was planning. I wanted to figure this out on my own and then present it to Jeremy.

Jeremy

I was in the garage working on Katie's broken bicycle when I heard Tess yell at the kids. I love my kids; I do. But, man, do they drive me crazy at times. They also remind me of my older sister, Jen, and me. We were always calling each other names, and I was always doing things to piss her off. I'd sing a song she hated over and over or I'd put rubber bugs in her favorite box of cereal. I never thought we'd like each other when we grew up. Turned out we get along really well. Hell, she's even my office manager.

I wondered what Tess was being so secretive about. I thought about sneaking onto her computer. Maybe check the history to see what websites she had visited. But as much as I wanted to do this, I knew if she found out she'd be pissed. She'd think I didn't trust her. I kind of wondered if there was another guy, but I knew Tess, and she'd never cheat on me. It was the one thing she'd made clear early-on in our dating.

She had a boyfriend for a couple of years before we met. Turned out he'd been cheating on her. When Tess caught him she wasn't heartbroken because she knew the relationship had gone south, but she was furious he hadn't ended their relationship before starting a new one. She said she'd never do that.

I went back to fixing Katie's bike. I always loved fixing things, and it killed me I didn't seem to be able to fix my marriage. I never loved anyone like I love Tess, but I could feel her drifting away a little more each day.

Even though we were back sleeping in the same bed, we still weren't together physically or emotionally. I felt as if I was treading water in the ocean and being hammered by big waves while trying to keep from drowning. And damn it, I was tired of treading.

Tess

The expo center was crowded. Jeremy and I had never been at the builders' show before, so I wasn't sure what to expect. The kids were staying with Jeremy's parents. They didn't want to come, which was good. It seemed like all they did anymore was fight, and I didn't feel like having to play cop. I wanted to be able to enjoy the show.

There were rows and rows of vendors selling everything from patio pavers to windows to vinyl siding. We found a lot of builders and contractors who specialized in home renovation.

There was one builder Jeremy wanted to make sure we checked out. He had made some calls and several people recommended Yorktowne Builders. It was a family-owned business that had been in the area since it began sixty years ago.

Jeremy opened the brochure he'd picked up when we walked in the door. He pointed to a layout with numbered squares. "It looks like Yorktowne is right here." He pointed to a block numbered 172. "So it's two rows over."

I followed Jeremy, weaving through the crowd. Along the way we ran into a couple of his patients who, of course, insisted on chatting.

"I just love your husband," old Mrs. Mulberry said. "Of course, I loved his father. Was sad to see him retire. But Jeremy does a good job."

Jeremy smiled. "Thank you, Mrs. Mulberry."

"And I like the new hygienist you hired. Very attractive. Can't believe she has a teen-age daughter. She doesn't look more than a teen herself. Shame about her husband and all."

Jeremy nodded, and we made it past Mrs. Mulberry.

"You didn't tell me you hired a new hygienist," I said.

"I didn't think it was important. Besides, you don't tell me things."

"What's that supposed to mean?"

"Just how it sounds. You don't tell me what you're doing on the computer all the time."

"That's not fair."

"Look, Tess. I don't want to fight. And it is fair. You don't tell me things, so why should I tell you things. What's that saying? What's good for the goose is good for the gander?"

I grunted. I definitely didn't want to get into a fight in front of booth number 172. We walked over to the booth and a tall, dark-haired man turned around. He was gorgeous, and I recognized him immediately. It was Cole from cycle class.

Chapter 11

Jeremy

When the man turned around, I saw by the way his eyes widened and his smile he recognized Tess.

"Hi, Tess," he said. "I almost didn't recognize you without your gym clothes on."

Tess's face turned flamingo pink, and she smiled. "Hi, Cole. This is my husband, Jeremy. Jeremy, this is Cole. He's in my cycle class."

I extended my hand to shake his. "Hi. I've heard a lot about that cycle class. I'm going to have to try it sometime."

Cole pointed to me. "Well, from what I understand, Tess will soon be teaching, so you'll have to check out her class. She works harder than anyone I know in class."

Tess's face turned a deeper shade of pink.

"So, what can I do for you?" Cole asked.

"We're interested in building an addition," I said. "Yorktowne Builders has been highly recommended."

"That's good to hear," Cole said. "We've been around for six decades. My great-grandfather started the business. I'm the third generation to be involved."

"So you run the company?" Jeremy asked.

"Pretty much. My dad is semi-retired."

"I see."

"Tell me what you have in mind," Cole said.

I noticed when Cole spoke, he looked at Tess and me, shifting his gaze between us. I knew that would be a plus in Tess's book. The last builder we'd talked to looked at me the entire time, and Tess was furious. When we walked away, she called him a "complete idiot" and said she wouldn't contract with him if he was the last builder on earth.

"What is it about some men?" she said. "It's like they think my opinion doesn't matter, that I have no say? I mean, I was standing right in front of the dick, and he acted like I wasn't there."

I briefly explained to Cole what I was looking for. "Of course, I'm open to ideas."

"Probably the best place to start is for me to come to your house and check out the property, take some measurements and go from there." Cole pulled up his appointment log on his laptop. "Okay, give me some dates and times that work for you."

"I think you should come when Jeremy is there," Tess said.

"Do you have Saturday appointments?" I asked. "During the week is pretty much out for me."

"Sure," Cole said. "Whatever works for the client. How about next Saturday?"

I looked at Tess.

Tess checked the calendar on her phone. "It looks like Saturday will work. How about one?"

"One works for me," Cole said. "I guess we have a date."

Tess

I couldn't believe when the tall man turned around it was Cole. God, he was even more gorgeous in his dark suit, white shirt and red power tie. If Hillary had seen him dressed like this it would've made her pant even harder than she does in cycle class. The woman would like nothing more than to fuck Cole every which way, or so she's told everyone in the locker room. My guess is it pisses her off that Cole's not interested. I get the feeling that what Hillary wants, she gets.

I wasn't expecting Cole to make my insides tickle, and I didn't like that someone ten years younger could make me feel this way. I was definitely attracted to him, and that scared me. I've never been attracted to anyone since I started dating Jeremy. Not that I don't look at guys, but none has made my insides flutter. For the first time, I found myself wondering what it would be like being with another man. And I never wondered that, not even once, since Jeremy came into my life. I felt horrible even thinking such thoughts. I wasn't a tramp. And I'd never screw around on Jeremy. But I felt like I was cheating on him even thinking about it.

When Cole suggested coming to the house to take measurements, I thought it best Jeremy be there. It's not that I didn't trust myself, but I didn't like the effect Cole had on me. And with how I'd been feeling about Jeremy, I didn't want to be alone with Cole. There was obviously a mutual attraction. I felt it, and I was pretty sure Cole felt it, too.

"Cole seems like a nice young man," said Jeremy as we walked away from the booth.

I noticed how he stressed the word "young" as if he were trying to make a point.

"Yes, he is. I had no idea he was a builder. Funny the stuff you don't know about your gym buddies."

"Do you have other gym buddies I don't know about?"

"Not really," I said, ignoring that he stressed 'buddies'. "I pretty much just keep to myself."

"Except Cole."

"Except Cole what?"

"You talk to him."

"Look, Jeremy. I'm not sure what you're insinuating."

"I'm not insinuating anything. You must feel guilty about something if you think I'm insinuating something."

"I don't feel guilty about anything. I have nothing to feel guilty about. I met Cole in cycle class. His cycle was next to mine. End of story."

"Do you want to stop and get a bite to eat on the way home?" Jeremy asked.

"No, you just killed my appetite. I want to go home."

"Come on, Tess. Quit acting stupid."

"Stupid? Stupid? Do you think I'm acting stupid? You're the one who's acting like a dick!"

We were right outside the entrance to the expo center, and I noticed people were looking at us but I didn't care.

"Tess," Jeremy whispered. "Be quiet. People are looking."

I rolled my eyes and walked toward the car.

Jeremy

Sometimes Tess drives me crazy. Like now. She's pissed because I asked about Cole. But why should she be pissed if there's nothing between them? I know Tess wouldn't cheat, but I know guys and Cole seemed definitely interested in Tess. I could tell by the way his eyes lingered when he looked at her.

By the time I reached the car, Tess was already inside. I slipped behind the wheel and eased out of the parking space.

"Well, aren't you glad we came?" I asked.

Tess didn't say anything.

"So you're going to give me the silent treatment now?"

Still, she didn't speak.

I stopped the car and looked at her. "Okay. I'm sorry. I didn't mean to insinuate anything."

Tess looked at me. "Apology accepted. Let's start over. Yes, I'm glad we came. I'll be interested in seeing what Cole comes up with. But remember, I'm not one hundred percent convinced now is the time to add the room. I've agree to explore options, but I haven't agreed to build now."

I nodded. "Now, do you want to get a bite to eat?"

"Yes, I'm starving."

I smiled.

"What's so funny?" Tess asked.

"You were willing to starve instead of get something to eat because you were pissed at me."

"I wouldn't have starved. I would've gone home and eaten a peanut butter sandwich."

"Okay, then. You were willing to eat a peanut butter sandwich rather than get something you really wanted because you were pissed at me."

"Yeah. That sounds about right."

"Women," I said. "You really are crazy."

Tess

"So what are you hungry for?" Jeremy asked.

"That's a tough question. Not sure."

We were driving down the highway, passing restaurant after restaurant. Nothing really appealed to me.

"Sushi? Mexican? Thai?" Jeremy asked.

"Mexican sounds good. We haven't had Mexican in a while."

We pulled into the restaurant and walked inside.

"Would you like to sit at a booth or a table?" the hostess asked.

"Booth, please," I said.

We followed her to our table.

"Looks like we had perfect timing," said Jeremy, pointing to the growing crowd in the waiting area.

The waitress brought salsa and a basket of warm tortilla chips. "Would you like to place a drink order?"

I nodded. "A margarita with no salt on the rim," I said. "And a glass of water with a wedge of lemon."

"Same for me," Jeremy said. "Except I want the salt."

I heard her voice before I saw her. It was Maniac Maggie. What was with running into cycle class people today?

"So this must be the lucky guy," said Maggie, walking over to the table.

I smiled. "Jeremy, meet Maggie, my cycle instructor. Maggie, this is my husband Jeremy."

Maggie smiled. "Did Tess tell you she's going to get certified to teach?"

Jeremy nodded. "That's what she says."

"About time, too," Maggie said. "I've been trying to get her to teach for months now."

Maggie looked at me. "I missed you the other day, Tess. First class you missed in a long time."

My heart started to race. Jeremy didn't know I hadn't gone to class, even though I pretended to go. I went to a meeting instead. I wasn't sure if Jeremy knew my schedule or if he'd put two and two together, so I just smiled and told Maggie I'd see her tomorrow.

"She seems like a nice woman," Jeremy said after she walked away.

"She is. But she's a tough instructor. Her class is definitely not a class for beginners."

"So you missed class?" Jeremy said.

I nodded. I was going to tell him I left because I didn't feel well, but I didn't want to lie. So I didn't say anything else, hoping Jeremy would drop it.

The waitress returned with our margaritas, and we placed our order—chicken enchiladas verde for me and chicken enchiladas and beef burrito combo for Jeremy.

Jeremy lifted his glass. "To a great future."

I lifted my glass and touched his, hoping he was right.

Chapter 12

Jeremy

Dad was showing Gina his vintage postcard collection when Mom cornered me in the kitchen.

"Katie says you two have been fighting," Mom said. "Is that true?"

I sighed. "Kids."

Mom pursed her thin lips. "They usually don't lie about that kind of stuff, Jeremy."

"Okay. It's true. We've been having some problems."

Mom patted my arm. "It happens to everyone. You're at the age when the kids are getting older and your lives are changing."

I rubbed my neck. "That's just it. I don't want things to change. I like things the way they are."

"But I take it Tess doesn't."

"No. She wants to work."

"But she does work," Mom said.

"Outside the home, Mom. She wants a job that she gets dressed up for and goes to every day."

"Oh. I see. And you don't want her to work."

"You didn't work."

"That's true. I didn't. But, my God, don't compare your mother with your wife, Jeremy."

"I'm trying not to. But I know how much I loved coming home from school and having you here. Mike's mom worked, and he always complained about going home after school to an empty house."

"And he turned out all right," Mom said. "In fact, he turned out more than all right."

"I know what you're saying, Mom. I do. I just don't know why Tess wants to work so much. She doesn't have to. People will think she has to."

Mom placed her hands on her hips. "Is that what's this is about? You're worried people will think she works because she has to?"

I shrugged. "Maybe. A little. Sort of."

"Jeremy," Mom said in a stern voice I hadn't heard since I was a teen. "Get over it. If your wife wants to work because it makes her feel more complete, the least you can do is support her. I try never to get involved in my children's marriages, but when I see one of you acting stupid, you damn well better believe I'm going to tell you about it."

Mom had a few other choice words to say before we were interrupted by Tess.

Tess

I found Jeremy in the kitchen with his mom, Diana. They looked like they were neck deep in a serious conversation. "Are you ready to go?"

Jeremy nodded. "I'll get the kids."

Once Jeremy was out of the room, Diana waved for me to sit at the table with her.

"Jeremy tells me you're looking for a job," Diana said.

"Oh he did, did he?"

"Well, actually, Katie mentioned you two were fighting, and when I asked Jeremy about it he said you wanted to work outside the home. And I told him if you wanted to work outside the home, he should support you."

"Thanks. I appreciate your support. I know one of the things Jeremy is concerned about is having someone in reserve if the kids are sick and need to stay home from school."

"I've told you both over and over I'd be glad to help out. All you have to do is ask."

"That's what I told him, but you know your son. He can be pretty stubborn."

"Can't say he doesn't come by that honestly. Still, a relationship takes work. Tess, you're like a daughter to me. Like I told Jeremy, couples go through rough times. Heaven knows Harry and I had our share of rough times."

"Really?"

"Of course. I don't know a couple who hasn't. The big thing is to communicate. Don't hide your feelings. You aren't always going to agree on everything, but you both need to respect how the other feels."

"Thanks. I'm not sure what kind of job I'm looking for. I'm exploring some different options."

Harry walked into the kitchen. "There's my best gal." He smiled and kissed Diana on the cheek.

His romantic gesture made me smile. "You two are the most romantic older couple I know."

Harry frowned. "Who you calling old? There's still a lot of spring left in this chicken."

Diana laughed. "That's not what that girl in the grocery store thought earlier today. She thought your spring had sprung! Go ahead. Tell Tess about the stripper girl."

"There was a stripper in the grocery store?"

"Well, not quite," Harry said. "Although I wouldn't be surprised if she were in that line of work."

"So what happened?"

Harry rubbed his bald head. "Well, Diana and I were in the checkout line at the grocery store."

"I was reading a magazine," Diana interrupted.

Harry looked at Diana. "Are you telling this story or am I?"

Diana mashed her lips together.

Harry looked back at me. "We were in line when Peroxide Girl wearing jeans that had more holes than Swiss cheese walked toward us."

"And she had a tight shirt on," Diana jumped in.

Harry glared at Diana.

"Well, you didn't mention the tight shirt and that's an important detail."

Harry looked back at me. "Yes, big knockers stuffed into a shirt that looked like it was made for a puppy."

"And piercings," Diana said. "Lots and lots of piercings. And black nails."

Harry made a mean face at Diana.

Diana pretended to zip her mouth.

Harry continued. "All of the sudden the girl stops. Guess she could tell everyone was looking at her. It was hard not to. She was like a blue light special. She shouts, 'Why's everyone looking at me?' And she looked right at me, like she wanted me to answer. So I told her it was because she was the color of a carrot, which she was. Next thing I knew everyone was laughing."

"Everyone but her," Diana said. "The girl had obviously worked hard on her fake tan."

I laughed. "So what did the girl do?"

"She pointed to me and said, 'I'd rather be orange than old.' And she walked away."

We laughed and when Jeremy returned, Harry repeated the story.

Jeremy

Tess was quiet on the drive home, and the kids fell asleep. It's not often the car is this quiet. I was thinking about what Mom had said when I heard Tess stir.

Tess sat up and looked out the window. We were stopped at the square in town. "I didn't know the old bistro building was for sale," she said.

"It was just listed. I noticed it the other day on my way home from work."

"I always loved that place—the exposed brick walls and wooden ceiling beams and the old stone hearth that's big enough to stand in. I wonder what business will go in there?"

The light turned green, and I slowly drove by it. "Hopefully something good."

I could tell by the way Tess bit her lower lip and stared she had something on her mind.

"So what are your plans for tomorrow?" I asked.

"Going to cycle class, then I might do some job searching."

My cell phone rang. It was on the console between us. "Can you answer that?"

Tess picked up the phone. "Hello? Oh, Mike. It's you. Is everything okay? You sound excited."

Tess leaned toward me. "He took Gina to the hospital. Says she's having contractions."

"Let me talk to him." Tess handed me the phone.

"Do you want me to come to the hospital?" I asked Mike.

"Okay. Keep us posted. And, Mike, good luck. Tell Gina we're thinking of her and the baby."

I ended the phone call. "I don't think I've ever heard Mike sound so nervous. I hope everything goes okay."

"Yeah," Tess said. "I never went early. In fact, I was late with both of ours."

"Do you ever think about having another one?" I asked.

"Sometimes. But never for very long. Katie and John fighting all the time makes me realize two is enough."

"My sister and I were the same way. We fought all the time. But now look at us. Good friends. I even like her enough to let her run my office."

Tess smiled. "That's true. You and Jen are good friends. I hope one day John and Katie will be."

Tess

"You're on my side," Katie said.

"Mom, she kicked me," John said.

"I kicked you because you were on my side." Katie said.

I turned around. "Stop fighting! We're almost home. Each of you stay on your own side and don't touch one another."

I sighed. "So much for good friends."

Jeremy laughed. "Believe me, it'll take another decade or two until that happens."

When we returned home, the kids got their showers and went to bed. Jeremy checked in with Mike before calling it a night, but there was no news. I grabbed my laptop and went to find a cozy spot on the couch. I was interested in the old bistro property. I wondered about its list price. Maybe I'd check it out tomorrow after cycle class. No harm in looking, I thought.

I also did some research on Yorktowne Builders. There were photos of completed renovations, which included before and after photos, on its website. The work was impressive. And it didn't just renovate homes, it also renovated commercial spaces.

I couldn't wait to meet with my mentor Richard. I was excited to share my ideas and see what he thought. We planned to have dinner tomorrow night. I would just tell Jeremy I was going to the gym, but secretly I'd meet my mentor Richard. If things went well, then I'd talk to Jeremy about my plans and our future.

Chapter 13

Jeremy

As soon as I woke up, I checked my voicemail to see if there was a message from Mike. There wasn't. I thought I'd check in with him after I showered and ate breakfast.

Tess was already on her second cup of coffee when I stumbled into the kitchen. "What time did you go to bed last night?"

"I fell asleep on the couch. I was up late reading."

"Reading anything interesting?"

"I looked up some stuff about Yorktowne Builders. There's a photo gallery on its website of work they've done. It's pretty impressive."

I poured some granola into a bowl. "Do you like living here?"

"Of course," Tess said. "Why would you ask that?"

"Sometimes I wonder if we should build a new house. You know, instead of constantly fixing up this one."

"But I thought you liked living here?"

"I do. But when I think of sinking thousands of dollars into a major renovation, I wonder if it's worth it."

"You have a point. Let's just see what Cole comes up with. Maybe we won't like the plan or the price. By the way, have you heard from Mike yet?"

"No. I thought I'd call him after breakfast."

"I checked my messages and no word from Sue yet, either."

As if almost on cue, my cell phone beeped. I had a text from Mike.

"Damn," I said.

"What's wrong?"

"Gina. She's having problems. Her blood pressure is up. They're going to do an emergency C-section."

I texted Mike back. Told him to call me if he needed anything.

Tess

While the kids ate breakfast, I talked to Sue. She told me Gina went to the hospital yesterday after her water broke. She wasn't progressing, so they gave her Pitocin to induce labor, but her blood pressure shot up and she felt nauseated and vomited.

I told Sue to let me know if there was anything she needed me to do. Katie overheard my end of the conversation. "Is Gina going to be okay?"

I nodded. "I think so. Probably by the time you get home from school the baby will have been born."

"I hope it's a girl," Katie said.

"Bleh!" John said. "Too many girls."

I sipped my coffee. "Jack doesn't care if he gets a brother or a sister."

"Maybe we can swap if he gets a brother," John said.

Katie stared John down. "Pig face."

"Monkey breath."

"Stop it!" I yelled. "No name calling."

"She started it."

"Did not."

"Did, too."

"Go. Both of you. Get your backpacks and get to the bus stop."

As soon as the kids were out the door, I took off for the gym. I wanted to talk to Maggie about instructor training.

Jeremy

I checked the schedule when I got to work. It was packed. And old Mrs. Harris, who still thinks of me as a snotty nosed kid, was my first appointment. Great way to start off a Monday. The old woman always complained about my prices; she thinks she should get everything for damn near nothing.

I walked into the room to examine her teeth after the dental hygienist told me she was ready to be checked.

"There you are," said Mrs. Harris, grabbing my arm as I walked past the chair. "How's your mom?"

"She's well. I'll tell her you asked about her."

"Are you still with your wife?"

Sandy, my dental hygienist, coughed.

I put down the X-rays and turn to Mrs. Harris. "What did you just ask me?"

"I asked you if you were still with your wife."

Sandy, who was standing behind Mrs. Harris, mashed her lips together and rolled her eyes.

"The last time I checked I was," I laughed.

"Good. That's good. Because when I saw her out to dinner with that older man the other night, I was worried. Their heads were really close, and they looked like they were having a serious conversation."

I tried to keep from looking surprised. "Well, you have nothing to worry about."

I checked Mrs. Harris teeth. "We talked about gingivitis before. Make sure you're flossing every day and using antiseptic mouthwash."

"Do you know how expensive floss is?" Mrs. Harris said.

"I'll tell you what: Sandy will make sure you get a bag full of samples to take home. That should hold you over for a while, and you won't have to buy any."

Mrs. Harris patted my hand. "That's why I like coming to you. You understand what it's like being on a fixed income. Do you think she could throw some extra toothpaste samples in the bag, too?"

I nodded and glanced at Sandy, who was filling a bag with floss samples. "Hear that Sandy?"

"I'm on it," she said, stuffing a handful of small boxes of toothpaste into the bag.

I bolted from the room as soon as I could and went into my office to take a deep breath and collect my thoughts. Mrs. Harris' revelation bothered me. What was Tess keeping from me? Do I confront her about what Mrs. Harris said or let it go? I wasn't sure what to do.

Tess

I felt him before I saw him; Cole slipped in next to me in cycle class.

"Hi, Tess. It was great seeing you yesterday."

I could see Hillary, who was sitting in front of me, lean back so she could hear our conversation better.

"It was nice seeing you, too. I almost didn't recognize you."

Cole laughed. "Yeah. I can't wait to see you again. I have a million ideas of what we could do. I can't wait to share them with you."

"Great. I've liked everything you've done so far. I'm sure you'll be able to wow me when we get together."

The music started and Maniac Maggie hopped on her cycle seat. "Let's get ready people. You shouldn't be talking. If you're talking, you're not working hard enough."

I became lost in the music as my legs became a blur.

"Add resistance!" Maggie shouted. "Push through it people!"

I added resistance and visualized the hill Maggie was describing.

"Dig, people!" Maggie yelled. "You're not going to get to the top unless you dig. You've got to want it. Come on. We're all doing this together. Add more resistance."

"Ugh!" Hillary moaned.

"Can we stand yet?" someone in front yelled.

"Not quite," Maggie said. "Almost."

I felt as if I was riding through thick mud. The more resistance we added the harder it was to pedal.

"Okay, add more resistance and stand."

I pushed the resistance lever the rest of the way down and stood. I threw my weight from side to side as I pushed through the pain.

I could see Cole out of the corner of my eye. He was going twice as fast as I was. But it made me want to go faster, so I tried to match his speed.

"That's it, Tess," whispered Cole. "Keep up with me. Let's finish together."

Jeremy

I called Mike the first break I had. He and Gina had a daughter, and he was over the moon about it.

"Daisy is beautiful," Mike said.

I could hear the excitement in Mike's voice. They named the baby after Gina's great-grandmother.

"And Gina was incredible," Mike said. "God, I love her so much. I still can't believe all of this has happened to me."

"You deserve it, Mike. After all these years, you guys are finally together, having the family you always wanted."

"Thanks. How are things with Tess?"

"We'll catch up later," I told him. "My next patient's here. Tell Gina I said congratulations, and if you need anything call me."

I wanted to tell Mike about what Mrs. Harris told me and get his advice on how to handle the situation, but I didn't want to be a downer on one of the most important days of his life. I figured we'd connect later.

My sister Jen walked into my office. "It was a girl, right?"

"How'd you know?"

"Just a lucky guess."

"Well, Mike is on cloud nine. I don't think I've ever heard him sound so excited."

"Well, he's been waiting pretty much his whole life for this," Jen said.

"Yeah, guess you're right."

Jen laid some paperwork on my desk. "Mom told me about your talk last night."

"Surprise! Surprise!"

"What's that supposed to mean?"

"It means you and Mom tell each other everything."

"Do not."

"Do, too."

"Anyway, I think you should support Tess if she wants to work. I work, and you don't have a problem with that."

"Yeah, but you're my sister, not my wife."

"Yeah, and I can still kick your ass, so be good to your wife so I don't have to."

Jen left the room, and I texted Tess to tell her about Daisy, just in case she hadn't already heard.

Tess

When I walked into the locker room after class, Hillary and some other women were huddled in the corner. I could tell by their whispers and glances in my direction they were talking about me.

I opened my locker to get my soap and shampoo.

Hillary walked over and stood beside me. "You and Cole seem to be getting pretty chummy."

"Not really," I said.

"Not that I was eavesdropping or anything, but it sounded like you two might have a thing."

I turned to face her. "What the fuck are you talking about, Hillary?"

"Fucking. That's what I'm talking about. Are you doing him?"

"Oh, Christ! I'm not even going to answer that question."

"Then you are, aren't you?"

"Hillary, I'm married."

"So?"

"So I would never do that to Jeremy."

"What makes you think he's not doing it to you?"

"Because I know him."

"Do you?" she asked.

"Is there something you know that I don't know?"

"Maybe."

"What are you insinuating?"

"It's just that...well, I really shouldn't say."

"No, by all means, say. You've already started, so you might as well finish."

She sighed. "I would just ask him about his new dental hygienist. That's all I'm going to say."

And she walked away, swinging her hips from side to side.

I stayed in the shower a long time. I was afraid if I saw Hillary in the locker room I'd punch her perfect face.

I got Jeremy's text after I showered and decided to stop at the department store to buy Daisy some pink outfits. I needed something to cheer me up. And now that we knew the baby was a girl, she definitely needed some pink things. And maybe a baby doll and purse. And shoes—definitely shoes.

Chapter 14

Jeremy

My afternoon flew by. Renee, my new dental hygienist, seemed to be settling in. This was the start of her second week, and I was pleased with her work. Jen had interviewed a number of applicants before I interviewed her top four choices. I picked Renee, but honestly I would've been happy with any one of them.

While the day started with Mrs. Harris, one of my worst patients, it ended with one of my favorites—Mr. Hamme. Mr. Hamme was as happy as Mrs. Harris was miserable. Too bad the two of them couldn't get together. They'd balance each other out. They were both widowed and about the same age. Maybe I should suggest it.

Mr. Hamme flashed his toothy grin as I walked into the room. "How's my boy?"

"I'm great, Mr. Hamme, especially since you're my last patient of the day."

"You know what they say: Save the best for last."

I smiled. "Having any problems?"

"I've been constipated lately. Darn bowels don't work as well as they once did. And when I pee, it sprays everywhere."

I coughed. "I meant with your teeth. Are you having any problems with your teeth?"

Mr. Hamme waved his hand. "Oh! No, boy. It's about the only thing I'm not having problems with. Even the ladies like my new dentures, so I smile a lot."

He winked and flashed a wide smile.

"Is Mrs. Harris one of those ladies by any chance?"

"That old coot that lives on Harding Street?"

"I believe that's the one."

"She's a busybody. Always coming into the senior center telling people what to do. And she complains about everything. She gives me the willies. Why'd you ask?"

"No reason," I said. "She was my first patient today. I just thought you might know one another."

"We do, and I wish we didn't."

So much for the idea of suggesting they date, I thought.

I examined Mr. Hamme's teeth. "Everything looks good. If you have any problems call me."

"About my teeth or anything?"

I laughed. "Since I'm your dentist, about your teeth. But if you really get in a fix and need to call me about something else, that's okay, too."

"Good to know, son. Good to know. An old man like me just might need a youngin' like you down the road."

Tess

When I returned home, I wrapped Daisy's gifts and put a casserole in the oven. I was supposed to meet Richard at six. Cassie was coming over to babysit; Jeremy had a Rotary Club meeting. I think I had everything covered.

I called Sue, and she said Gina and Daisy were doing great. Daisy had dark hair like Mike and a lot of it. She weighed six pounds and was nineteen inches long. Sue said Gina didn't want to put Daisy down. That made me smile. I remember those days when all I wanted to do was cuddle.

I remember rocking Katie and John when they were babies, their tiny fingers wrapping around mine. I thought they were perfect in every way. Hard to believe they turned into such mouthy kids.

I figured I'd give Gina a few days before I popped over to visit. Sue told me Mike had taken the rest of the week off, so I knew she'd have help.

John beat Katie home from school and loaded up on snacks.

"Don't eat too much or you'll spoil your dinner."

He sat at the table. "What are we having anyway?"

"Pasta and hamburger casserole."

"With lots of cheese melted on top?"

I nodded. "With loads of cheese."

Katie walked in as John finished his cheese stick. She dropped her bags and headed for the refrigerator. She opened the door, peeked inside and turned around. "Did you eat the last cheese stick?"

John nodded.

"Pig."

"I didn't see your name on it."

"But I like cheese sticks more than you. You only ate it because it was the last one."

"Did not."

"Did, too."

I took a deep breath. "Not now, you two. Finish your snacks and go do your homework. If you can't be nice to one another, stay away from each other. Remember, Cassie is babysitting. Both your dad and I have meetings."

"I'm not looking forward to being an adult," John said.

"Why?"

"Because all you do is have boring meetings—especially Dad."

"And when you're not meeting you're cooking and cleaning and washing clothes," Katie said.

I rolled my eyes and went upstairs to change. I wasn't sure what to wear to my meeting with Richard. I didn't want to be overdressed, but I knew he was coming right from work. I decided on tan slacks, a floral blouse and blazer.

No sooner had I changed when I heard Katie answer the door and let Cassie in. I looked into the mirror one last time. I hoped Richard liked what I had to show him.

Jeremy

The Rotary Club meeting was at the Washington Club, a couple blocks from the old bistro building Tess seemed overly interested in. Usually Keith and I go to the meeting together, but I still felt a little awkward about what happened, so I didn't call. He didn't either. But when we ran into each other, everything fell into place.

"Kris is so excited Gina had a girl," Keith said. "Went shopping already and bought a boatload of pink stuff."

I laughed. "Tess texted me; she did, too."

"When I talked to Mike, he seemed really excited."

I agreed. "He made me excited just listening to him. And getting up every two hours with a newborn is not something that excites me."

"I know what you mean. I'm glad we're done."

"Hell, you have an entire basketball team. I hope you're done."

Keith laughed. "I think the meeting's starting. We'd better grab a seat."

The president talked and talked and talked. I think the guy liked hearing himself speak. He went through the various community service projects and then discussed some international projects. The water project in Nicaragua seemed like a good one to get involved with.

"Jeremy," the president shouted. "Will you chair the scholarship committee this year?"

I jerked to attention. I felt as if I'd been caught daydreaming in class.

"Sure, but I'd like to have a co-chair."

Keith raised his hand. "I'll co-chair the committee."

"Fantastic," the president said. "We think we'll have enough to give four deserving seniors college scholarships this year, and there are usually a lot of applicants. Next on the agenda."

I nodded at Keith.

By the time the meeting was over, I was yawning every minute.

"Feel up to getting a beer?" Keith asked.

"Not tonight. It's been a long day. I'm heading home."

Tess

I saw Richard as soon as I entered the restaurant. He was an older man, maybe 60ish, with salt and pepper hair, blue eyes and an easy smile. He was tall and thin like Jeremy, and when I stood next to him I had to look up.

He held out his hand to shake mine. "Tess, good to see you again."

I smiled.

The restaurant wasn't busy, and Richard asked the hostess to seat us in a quiet area.

"Would you like the wine menu?" the server asked.

I held up my hand. "None for me, thank you."

Richard ordered a martini and some dinner. I was too nervous to eat, so I told him I'd eaten with the kids before coming.

"So, what did you come up with?"

"I like the idea of opening a tea room."

"And you think this will be a viable business in this economy?"

"I do. I think location is important. Perhaps locating it downtown near the historic district and tapping into the tourism market. People are touring the area and need a break, something different. I'll create a laid-back atmosphere in which they can escape the busyness, likewise for locals. And I could feature special events, like mom and daughter teas, or girl and doll teas."

Richard sipped his martini.

"Do you have a particular property in mind?"

"I'd love the old bistro building. And I love the idea of incorporating a gift shop into the space. I could sell not only tea-related items but other items as well. Maybe even sell locally made items, which I'm sure the tourists would be interested in. By diversifying my inventory, the gift shop could serve the non-tea crowd and be another source of income."

"Do you think the old bistro building will offer some semblance of tranquility?"

"I think with noise buffering walls, plants and the right furniture I can create a relaxing haven where when people walk inside, they feel as if they've entered a garden. I want unique, something that sets it apart."

"Would you buy a franchise?"

I shook my head. "I'd like to open my own."

"Well, you certainly seem to have the interpersonal skills for such a business. Are you prepared for the long hours?"

"I'm still working on that. But I'd definitely need help."

"And what are you seeing in terms of trends?"

"My research shows fruit and herbal teas have increased by thirty percent, and specialty teas, such as green tea, have grown fifty percent."

"How far are you on your business plan?"

I reached for my bag and pulled out a manila folder. "It's all there. The business plan, marketing plan, projected income and financial needs. I even worked on a menu."

Richard smiled. "Very good. I'll look this over and then we can meet again. In the meantime, work on finding local suppliers. And make sure you research which licenses and permits you need to open a tea room in the historic district."

I nodded. "I'll get on it right away."

"I like the idea of opening a business that puts money back into the community," Richard said.

"My thoughts exactly."

Chapter 15

Jeremy

On the way to my car, I took a detour to check out the bistro building. I remember the night I proposed to Tess. I was in dental school and we came home for the weekend to visit my parents. I took Tess to the bistro. I knew it was her kind of place. Kind of artsy with its exposed brick walls and panel ceiling and original wooden floors. The bistro also supported local artists by showcasing their work. Customers could buy the pieces.

We sat in the back booth, which was shaped like a U. It could seat six, but I asked the waitress if she'd give it to us. I was a regular before going away to college, so when I came home, Jackie, the waitress, always made sure I got top-notch service. I wanted the extra privacy, and with its high walls and flickering candle in the middle of the table, the booth was cozy and romantic.

I can't remember what we ate that night. I'm sure it was good. But I'll never forget what happened when Jackie brought the bill. Tess had this annoying habit of always grabbing the bill to look at it first. The bistro used old books instead of leather bill folders. In our past visits, Tess always enjoyed this particular aspect of the dining experience. She loves books, especially old ones, and always looked forward to seeing what book the bill was presented in.

"Are you sure you don't want any dessert?" Jackie had asked Tess.

Tess held her stomach. "I couldn't eat another bite."

"I guess that means we'll take the check," I told Jackie.

When Jackie returned, I thought I'd have to pick Tess off the floor. As soon as Jackie placed the book on the table Tess's eyes sprung out of their sockets.

She ran her hands over the cover of the book, which was Shakespeare's *Romeo and Juliet*. "Oh. My. God. This has to be old. It's beautifully aged."

"Yeah, it's no thrift store edition, that's for sure. My guess is it's a rare 1871 leather bound published by Scott Webster and Geary."

Tess flashed me a puzzled look. She opened the book to examine it further and the hefty price I paid for the book was worth it just to see the look on her face. She picked up the check, but there weren't any numbers on it. A diamond ring was taped to the slip with a note that said, "Will you marry me?"

Tess cried and I got down on my knees and she said yes and when Jackie saw the proposal was made and accepted, she announced it to all of the patrons. We ended up staying for a while because people kept buying us drinks.

God, I hadn't thought about that in years. We were so in love then, so happy. And like the book, I thought we'd be around for a long time.

"Are you sure you don't want something to drink?" Richard asked.

I sighed. "Well, maybe just one."

Richard called the server over, and I ordered a glass of white zinfandel. I guess I hadn't realized how nervous I was to share my research. When I first thought about starting my own tea room, there was so much I didn't know. But I've learned a lot from Richard, who volunteers his time to advise and mentor small business owners. I found him through a non-profit program administered by the Small Business Association. Having someone to talk to who's been in my shoes is a huge help. I appreciate his expertise and wisdom.

The server brought my wine, and I lowered my shoulders, trying to relax as much as I could.

"What's your biggest concern about this?" Richard asked.

I smiled. "Do I have to pick just one?"

He laughed.

"I suppose getting the start-up financing. My husband, Jeremy, wants to build an addition to our house. I haven't shared this idea with him yet. He knows I'm looking for a job, but he doesn't know I've been considering starting my own business. I want to have everything figured out before I talk to him. But I'm worried we won't have the money to sink into this if he has his mind set on the addition."

Richard sipped his martini. "So you might need some investors."

I nodded.

"I can't wait to read your plans more carefully," Richard said. "I do think it's a good idea to increase your income by selling retail products. Incorporating a gift shop into the plan is smart. Even if people don't want to come in and sit for a tea, they can shop in the store and buy tea, accessories, food products and other gifts. And I also like that you want to include locally made products in your inventory."

"I agree. Diversification is key. I also think offering tea tastings might be profitable."

"Any idea for a name?"

"I've been playing around with a few but haven't come up with any that completely wow me."

Richard took the last sip of his martini. "Picking a name is the fun part."

"And it's an important part. Any ideas come to mind?"

Richard smiled. "Maybe Tess's Tea Room. Simple and straight forward and the alliteration gives it a nice ring."

"Thanks. I'll add it to my list. Maybe the next time we meet I'll have some to share with you."

"In the meantime, I'll look over what you've given me, and you work on the new stuff I asked for tonight."

I laughed. "It's been a long time since I had this much homework."

Richard smiled. "But it's doing the homework that leads to success."

"That's what my mom used to say when I was in school. I hated homework, but she'd always remind me that we learn by doing the homework, so when we're tested we know exactly what to do."

"Your mom was a wise woman." Richard asked.

"Yeah. Try telling that to a teen who thinks she knows everything. It took me until my mid-twenties to realize how smart my mom and dad were."

Jeremy

I turned the corner and walked toward the bistro building. There weren't many people on the street. Like a lot of downtowns, retailers fled the city when malls popped up in the suburbs. There were a lot of empty storefronts that in their heyday were bustling places of commerce, but slowly the city was coming back through various initiatives aimed at revitalizing the downtown. It was great to see more and more independent shops opening. Together they created a vibrant arts district, which drew people into the city for special events.

I passed a homeless man who looked like a bundle of rags sitting on a bench. I stopped and gave him a twenty. His eyes lit up, and he muttered thank you and took off.

"Get something hot to eat," I yelled, hoping he wouldn't blow it on booze.

I stood in front of the bistro building, reading the For Sale sign in the window when I got a text from Tess.

"I'll be home soon. Are you still at the meeting?"

Just as I was about to text Tess back, I saw her walk around the corner—with another man.

My heart felt as if it had just been crushed by my fifty-pound barbells. When Tess saw me, her hand flew to her chest. I didn't know whether to tackle the guy or leave. I was too angry to even speak. A million thoughts ran through my head. I knew Tess had some sort of meeting tonight, but not with a man who looked old enough to be her father. And then I remembered what Mrs. Harris had said during her dental appointment, about seeing Tess with an older man and I wondered if this was him.

I ran my fingers through my hair. My face felt hot, and my heart beat out of control.

The man noticed something was obviously up. "Tess, what's wrong? Are you okay?"

I didn't wait for her answer. I turned around and ran, anxious to get as far away from them as I could. I'd seen enough.

Tess

When I saw Jeremy I felt like the biggest jerk around. All I was trying to do was get everything in order before I shared my idea with him. But, coupled with all of our recent problems, I knew seeing me with another man gave him the wrong impression. I felt as if I'd stabbed him in the heart. And as mad as I'd been at him lately, I wouldn't intentionally do that. Obviously, I never expected to run into him downtown. How was I going to explain it to Jeremy? And even when I did, would he believe me?

"Who was that?" Richard asked.

I sighed. "My husband."

Richard cleared his throat. "Well, then. Maybe you better get home. By the look on his face, I think you have some explaining to do. And if he'd like to talk with me, I'd be glad to meet with him."

"Thanks, Richard. But it's my fault. I should've been upfront with him about this from the start, but I really wanted to do this on my own."

"Keeping secrets is never good," Richard said. "Secrets have a way of coming out just when you don't want them to."

I couldn't get to my car fast enough. All I could think about was getting home to talk to Jeremy. I called Sue because I figured Jeremy would call Mike the first chance he had. And I wanted Sue to know the truth because I knew Mike would tell Gina and Gina would tell Sue. Sue could straighten everyone out. She's good at that kind of stuff and everyone listens to her.

Tom answered the phone.

"Tom, is Sue there? I really, really, really need to speak with her."

"Sure. I'll get her."

I pulled out of the city parking garage and almost hit the brick wall.

"Damn," I muttered.

"Tess, are you okay?" Sue asked. "You sound upset."

I started crying and everything flooded from my mouth. Me wanting a job and exploring the possibility of opening my own business. Finding Richard through a non-profit mentoring program that pairs successful business owners with newbies. Our meeting tonight and walk to the bistro and seeing Jeremy standing on the street in front of it.

"Okay, calm down. Take a deep breath. Where are you now?"

"Headed home. Cassie's babysitting the kids, and I promised her I wouldn't be late because it's a school night."

"Would it help if I came over? Cassie could go home and maybe you and Jeremy could go somewhere to talk quietly. Just the two of you."

"Would you do that?"

"Of course I'll do that. This all sounds like a big misunderstanding. But I also know Jeremy and you and when it comes to fighting, you two are champs at it. No sense on waking the kids up and getting them upset."

"But where would we go?"

"I'll bring the keys to our cabin by the river. It's only a half-hour away. You can go there and talk and, if you're lucky, make up. I can spend the night. Go ahead and pack a bag for both of you just in case."

I sniffed. "Thanks Sue."

"See you soon."

Chapter 16

Jeremy

I sped out of the city and headed in the opposite direction of where I lived. I wasn't sure where to go, but I knew I didn't want to go home. Tess and I would end up fighting, and I needed time to think. I slammed my palm against the steering wheel. Damn Tess. How could she do this to me? Another man explains why Tess had become so distant. And here I thought it had to do with her wanting to work and me not wanting her to. Shows how much I know.

I pulled into a bar I hadn't been to in ages. In my younger days, before I was old enough to legally drink, Mike and I would come here and get served. We thought we were hot stuff back then. I bellied up to the bar and asked for a beer. As I sipped the beer, a girl walked in that was all cleavage and hair products. She sat two stools down.

"Usual, Stella?" the bartender asked.

She nodded, and he slid a draft in front of her.

"So what's your story, cowboy?" Stella asked.

I took a sip of my beer. "Don't have one."

"A guy like you doesn't come in a dump like this unless he's trying to bury some sorrows."

I didn't answer.

"Well, my name's Stella."

I nodded. I really didn't want to get into a conversation with Stella. I didn't feel like talking to anyone.

She tapped her long red fingernails on the bar. "So, guess you're not going to tell me your name. Well, okay then I'll just have to call you No-Name."

I couldn't help but smile. The woman was persistent. "It's Jeremy."

Stella sipped her beer. "Jeremy. That's a nice name. I had an ex who was named Jerry. The only good thing about Jerry was his paycheck—when he felt like working, which wasn't too often.

"Then there was Henry; we called him Hank. Hank was better than Jerry when it came to the paycheck part, but he couldn't keep his dick in his pants. Turned out he was dipping it in every broad in town. Thank God I dumped him before he gave me herpes. The ones who came down the line weren't so lucky. Hank had started a mini epidemic in this town. People called him Herpes Hank."

I coughed. The lady was a trip. And her mouth ran like commode water when the stopper isn't working.

"Take my advice, cowboy. Go home. Straighten it out. It can't be that bad."

I threw a twenty on the counter and hopped off the stool. "See you around, Stella."

She waved her hand. "No you won't, but that's okay. I'm dragging up. Headed south. Gonna find me husband number six."

Tess

When I got home I tried to act as if nothing was wrong. The kids were in bed and I paid Cassie, reminding her about babysitting on Saturday. But just as I said it, I realized I might not need her. From the look on Jeremy's face, I couldn't imagine him wanting to go anywhere with me—especially to a charity event at the club where we'd be surrounded by people who always seem to know the worst about you.

I changed and packed bags like Sue had suggested. If Jeremy came home, I'd convince him to go to Sue's cabin to talk.

I told Sue I'd leave the back door open and to just come in. When I came downstairs after packing, she was sitting at the kitchen table.

"Thanks for coming," I said.

"Not a problem. Have you heard anything yet?"

"Not a word. How about Mike or Tom?"

"No. Tom talked to Mike earlier. He didn't mention it to Mike and Mike didn't say anything to him, so my guess is Jeremy hasn't told anyone."

"I just wish I knew where he is."

Sue pursed her lips. "I did keep an eye out for his car on the way over, just in case. But I didn't see it."

I filled Sue in on my tea house idea and my mentorship with Richard.

"If you would've seen Jeremy's face when he saw Richard and me together, it was awful. But I can see why he jumped to conclusions. I was so stupid to keep this from him, but I wanted to do it on my own, to show him I didn't need him."

I couldn't keep from crying.

Sue hugged me.

"I should've run after him, but I was so stunned nothing would come out of my mouth, so that made it even worse."

"Did you text or try calling him?"

"Of course. But he doesn't answer."

"Want me to try?"

"No. You've done enough. Guess I'll just have to wait and hope he comes home soon. He can't stay away forever. He has to work tomorrow."

Jeremy

I left the bar, drove for a while and pulled into a hotel. I needed to get some sleep. Tess had called several times and sent some texts, but I just wasn't ready to see her or talk to her. I thought maybe things would look better in the morning.

I didn't have a change of clothes, but that was the least of my problems. I knew it was a busy week at the office, and my first appointment was at 8. Hopefully none of the girls would notice I wore the same clothes two days in a row.

I didn't see who was behind the counter before it was too late. It was nosey Mrs. Geesey from church. She apparently works the night desk. "Something to do," she explained to me at check-in.

Her squinty eyes peered over the top of her wire-rimmed glasses. "No bags?"

I shook my head.

"There's complimentary soap and shampoo in the rooms," she explained. "You can pick up a toothbrush and toothpaste at the store across the street."

"Thanks," I said. "That's good to know."

I wasn't about to offer any kind of explanation, although Mrs. Geesey seemed to be waiting for one. She handed me the room key, and I headed for the elevator.

"The store's open all night," she yelled. "They also have disposable razors and shaving cream."

I nodded and stepped into the elevator, eager to get away from Mrs. Geesey. I was sure she'd be on the phone to my mom the first chance she had. That's how it goes in a small town. Your secrets are never secret. Someone always knows something they're not supposed to.

When I got to the room, I turned on the TV and plopped on the bed. The last time I spent a night in a hotel was last summer when we took the kids to Disney World. We usually go every year and stay at the Polynesian. Tess loves it there. She suggested we renew our vows at the resort's Sunset Pointe on our 20th anniversary.

I punched the bed. "Damn, Tess!" I knew our marriage wasn't great, but I never thought Tess would screw around behind my back. I'd at least think she'd be more careful. I mean, walking down a city street isn't exactly keeping an affair under wraps, unless...

I ran my fingers through my hair. What if it wasn't an affair? They weren't holding hands. The guy didn't have his arm around her. And he did look about twenty years older.

I turned on my cell phone. There was a text from Tess. It said, "It's not what you think. Richard is my business mentor. Let me explain."

"What the hell is she talking about? Business mentor?"

I turned off the phone. I needed some sleep. Maybe things would look better in the morning.

Tess

I woke up on the couch to an infomercial for a wearable towel, which seemed as stupid as those blankets with sleeves. I looked over at Sue, who'd fallen asleep on the recliner. I figured Jeremy wasn't coming home. It was too late. I turned off the TV and went to bed. I didn't want to wake up Sue, so I let her alone.

I pulled back the sheets and crawled into bed. Where in the hell was he? I kept seeing the scene in my mind. Me walking with Richard. Looking up and seeing Jeremy. The hurt look on Jeremy's face. My head was killing me, and I couldn't sleep. I thought about taking a sleeping pill, but it was 2 in the morning. If I took one now I'd wake up in a fog. I decided to read instead.

I walked over to the bookshelf and reached for the first book I saw. It was *Romeo and Juliet*, the book Jeremy used when he proposed to me.

The memory made me smile. How did our lives get so out of whack? I thought back over the past few years. It seemed as though we'd lost touch with each other. We didn't do the very thing my mother had always preached—date nights to focus just on us. Everything was about the kids and meeting all of their needs. Running them to drum lessons and dance classes. Taking them to baseball games and choir rehearsals. I guess I thought there'd be time for us later, but we'd drifted apart.

Maybe that's another reason why I was hell-bent on working. The kids didn't need me as much, and I had less in common with Jeremy as the years unfolded. Before having kids, we used to do a lot of things together—go hiking, ride bikes, spend an entire day binge-watching our favorite TV show. And I couldn't remember the last time we had done any of those things.

It was one of those ah-ha moments that hit you over the head and jolt your brain awake. You think about things you haven't thought about in forever. I knew Jeremy didn't understand. As far as he was concerned everything was great. He was a good provider and gave us a more than a comfortable life. But I just didn't want him for the paycheck he brought home. I wanted him to be the man I'd fallen in love with, the man before kids and responsibilities. But maybe, I thought, I have to change, too. I mean, I'm certainly not the same woman he fell in love with.

I'm not foolish enough to think we can go back to being the kids we once were, but could we find that piece in each other that had been buried by parenthood, buried by years of living life going in separate directions? Maybe I'm a dreamer. Maybe this is what happens once your kids are older. Maybe this is as good as it gets. But something told me it didn't have to be this way. The question was, could we find our way back.

Chapter 17

Jeremy

As soon as I walked into the office and saw my sister's face, I knew she knew. Jen followed me into my office and closed the door.

I pushed aside the papers in the corner of my desk and sat. "How'd you find out?"

Jen crossed her arms. "You mean besides you coming to work in the same clothes you wore yesterday?"

"Yeah."

Jen sighed. "Mom called me."

I shook my head. "Figured Mrs. Geesey would call her the first chance she had."

"So what's up, little brother?"

I gave her the cliff notes.

"Look, Jeremy. It doesn't take a marriage counselor to know things haven't been great between you and Tess. I've seen it. Mom's seen it. Dad's seen it. Everyone has. But I don't think Tess would screw around behind your back. You know what I think?"

I sat up straighter. "No, but I'm sure you're going to tell me."

"I think you saw what you wanted to see. You saw Tess with another man, who from what I understand is her mentor..."

"That's another thing. Why the hell does she need a mentor? And for what?"

"Let me finish. I think you saw Tess with another man and made some wild assumptions, which is probably logical considering the state of your marriage. But you and I both know that's not what's wrong with your marriage. You jumped to that conclusion as a way of diverting blame."

"Okay, Miss Smarty Pants, then what's wrong with my marriage?"

"I think you know. And I think Tess knows, too. Your problem is you don't communicate. And if you don't communicate, you're never going to be able to get out of the tail-dive you're in."

"So what do you suggest?"

"The office is closed the rest of the week since all of the dental hygienists are going to training. I've arranged for you and Tess to go away for a few days. Just the two of you. No kids. Mom and Dad will watch John and Katie."

"What if Tess won't go?"

"I think she will. I've talked to Sue, who spent the night with Tess, and she's probably talking to her right about now. You leave tonight on a late flight to Key West."

"Key West?"

"Yep. It's where you spent your honeymoon."

"No shit, Jen. I know that. Is that why you picked it?"

"You liked it, right?"

"I loved it. Tess did, too."

"Then it's the perfect getaway."

"So this is like an intervention?"

"Call it what you want, little brother. I just hope it knocks some sense into both your heads."

Tess

"Key West?" I said. "That's where we spent our honeymoon."

Sue smiled. "Jen has it all figured out. You leave tonight. The only thing you have to do is pack your bags."

"Tonight? But what about the kids? I have to make arrangements."

Sue waved her hand. "Already taken care of. Jeremy's parents are watching them."

I sighed. I didn't know what to say. I loved Key West. It was one of the funniest places I'd ever visited. Jeremy and I always planned on going back, but like a lot of things it never happened.

"Look," Sue said. "I have to run. Call me if you need anything. Think about what I said. You need to talk to Jeremy."

"And he has to listen."

"You both have to listen," Sue said. "Don't let the good thing you have slip away without a fight."

I hugged Sue. "Thanks for coming over."

"Don't mention it. I just might need a favor one day."

"Anything. Just ask me for anything, and it's yours."

After Sue left, I went upstairs to pack. I had to admit, I was excited about going to Key West. There's nothing like a Key West sunset. Whether watching it from Mallory Square or aboard a sailboat or catamaran, it's absolutely stunning. Jeremy and I tried to catch it every night when we were there. One night, we went on the last snorkeling excursion of the day to the coral reef and caught the sunset on the way back.

I heaved the leather suitcase onto my bed. When I opened it I found Disney park maps from our trip last summer. I guess it was the last time I'd used the suitcase. I pulled out my black tankini. Despite working hard to get in shape, I still didn't feel confident enough to wear a bikini.

After I finished packing, I started to pack for Jeremy. He has the most boring wardrobe in the world. He wears nothing but tan cargo shorts, unless he's exercising and then he wears Nike nylon shorts.

I dashed off a quick email to Richard, explaining Jeremy and I were going away for several days. I told him I'd contact him when we returned. After listening to his mini lecture as he walked me to my car after running into Jeremy, I knew he'd approve.

Jeremy

I had to admit, I was excited about going to Key West. Tess and I hadn't taken a vacation as a couple since before we had kids. I smiled, remembering the jet ski tour we'd taken around the island. Tess was so pissed because she was thrown off when we hit the choppy Atlantic. She was sore, too, because her pelvic floor pounded against the seat as we flew through the water.

I wasn't happy Mrs. Geesey called Mom, but maybe the intervention is just what we needed. I hadn't realized until Jen said it that everyone knew Tess and I were having problems. I thought we'd done a pretty good job of concealing it. But, like Jen said, people aren't dumb. They see through the fog even when you're lost in it.

None of the other girls in the office said anything about wearing the same clothes two days in a row. I knew if they had noticed it, they'd probably mention it to Jen who'd control the office gossip.

I walked out of my office and past the check-in counter when the phone rang. I could tell from the conversation it was Mrs. Harris. She apparently called to complain her gums were sore from her visit yesterday.

"I'll take it." I told Jen. "Transfer it to my office."

I went back to my office and picked up the phone.

"Mrs. Harris, how is one of my favorite patients?"

"Terrible. My gums hurt. And that floss Sandy gave me is limp and slippery, and I don't like using it."

I inhaled, trying to figure out what to say so the conversation didn't drag on. "Are you using the antiseptic mouth wash to gargle?"

"Didn't see any mouthwash in the bag Sandy gave me."

"Yes. We have no samples of mouthwash. That's something you're going to have to buy."

"What? No samples of mouthwash? So you make my teeth hurt, and then you don't give me mouthwash to make it better. You make me buy the mouthwash to fix your mistakes."

"We didn't make any mistakes, Mrs. Harris. We cleaned your teeth. We removed all of the tartar and plaque. In order to have strong teeth and healthy gums, you need to brush your teeth after every meal, use floss and antiseptic mouthwash."

There was silence on the other end of the phone.

"Remember the time you called and you thought you had broken your tooth?" I asked.

She didn't answer.

"You came into the office and it wasn't your tooth, it was a large piece of tartar. If you don't take care of your teeth, the plague will eventually turn into tartar. So yesterday we removed all of that from your teeth. Yes, your teeth and gums might be a little sore. But if you adopt the dental habits I've asked you to, this wouldn't be a problem. Now, I have to go. My patient is waiting. Perhaps you ought to consider going to another dentist if you don't like the care you're receiving."

She slammed down the phone without saying a word. Maybe I finally shut the bitch up.

Tess

When the kids walked in the house after school, they saw the suitcases sitting by the door.

Katie plopped her backpack on the kitchen table. "Where are we going?"

"We aren't going anywhere. Your dad and I are going away for a few days. Just the two of us."

John punched the air. "Home alone here we come."

I smiled. "Think again. Grandma and Grandpa will soon be here. You'll stay with them, and they'll make sure you get to and from school and do your homework."

John hung his head. "Dang! It's never like it is in the movies."

As if on cue, John's grandparents walked in the door.

"There's my favorite grandkids," Harry said.

"We're your only grandkids," Katie said.

Diana looked at me. "Can we talk a minute?"

"Come on, kids," Harry said. "Let's go pack and give these two time to talk."

Harry, John and Katie bolted up the stairs.

"I hope you can work things out," Diana said. "Can I tell you a secret, something I've never told anyone?"

I nodded.

"Harry and I had trouble in our marriage, too. Things weren't always easy. There were times when I was lonely, being home with the kids all day. I resented he had this career, and I'd given up mine."

"You resented it? But Jeremy said you loved being a stay-at-home mom."

"Correction," Diana said. "Jeremy liked me being a stay-at-home mom. I did it because it was what Harry wanted and what was best for the kids, or so I thought. But it wasn't what was best for me. I felt as if I died a little each day and the more days that passed the more I resented my life. Of course, I didn't tell Harry how I felt. I kept it to myself. But I'd pretend to be other people. I'd create these characters and act them out as a way to turn what had been an ordinary life into an extraordinary one. It all seems so silly now, but it was my way of coping."

"So what happened?"

"In time, my fake world became my real world and I knew I needed help. It was a long road back. Harry helped."

"So he knew?"

"Eventually. You can't keep a secret like that from your husband forever. We went to counseling. Harry paid more attention to me and the kids. And I found an outlet for my creativity, which gave me a purpose."

"What sort of outlet?"

"I wrote. I began writing fiction. At first, it was short stories. Then I tried writing a novel."

"You wrote a novel?"

"Several," Diana said. "I'm Kristin Cavanaugh."

"The romance novelist?"

"The one and only."

"Oh. My. God. Does Jeremy know?"

"No one but Harry knows the true identity of Kristin Cavanaugh. And now you. I hope you'll keep it to yourself. Maybe when I'm dead it'll come out. And that's fine. I won't need to deal with the glares and whispers from women who obviously see me in a different light. But creating Kristin Cavanaugh saved me."

"Why are you telling me this?" I asked.

"Because I think you are where I was. And because I think you have an idea of what you'd like to do, but you're afraid to tell Jeremy. Am I right?"

I nodded. "I'd like to open a tea room. I've been meeting with a mentor from the Small Business Administration. I wanted to figure everything out before I talked to Jeremy about it."

"I think it's a wonderful idea," Diana said. "And Harry and I would love to be investors, when you get to that point."

"You'd do that?"

"I learned a long time ago to follow my heart and if this is where your heart is leading, follow it. But don't shut Jeremy out. You might just find he's a better partner than you had imagined."

I was stunned by what Diana had told me, and after they left I couldn't stop thinking about her being Kristin Cavanaugh. I'd read all of her books and, let's just say, they include a lot of X-rated parts. She's right. Her friends would definitely gossip if they knew she was Kristin.

Maybe Diana was right. Maybe my tea room could happen. And maybe Jeremy won't think it's such a stupid idea.

Chapter 18

Jeremy

When I got home, Tess had everything packed and ready to go. "Guess this is what you call an intervention."

Tess smiled. "Yeah, guess so. Look, Jeremy, I just want to get one thing straight before we leave. There is no other man. The man you saw me with is Richard Manning."

"Why does that name sound so familiar?"

"He owns the minor league baseball team and a string of successful restaurants and bars in the area."

"What the hell were you doing with him?"

"I tried to tell you but you took off."

"Do you blame me?"

I shrugged. "I guess not. But you didn't see what you thought you saw. He's been helping me with a business venture."

"God damn, Tess. You're thinking about starting a business and everyone else knows about it except me?"

"It's not like that. Only Richard. And Sue. I told her last night. That's it. No one else. I didn't want to tell you until I had it all figured out. Then I wanted to present my plan to you."

I sighed. "Did you ever stop to think I might want to be a part of it?"

"But you would be a part of it."

"That's not what I mean, and you know it. Whatever happened to us planning things together, to us figuring out life together?"

"We figured out going to Disney World together."

"Not exactly, Tess. You figured it out and ran it by me when you were done making all of the arrangements. I might've planned it a little differently."

"Then why didn't you say something?" Tess asked.

"Because it was too late. You already had everything booked. But you know what, if you had asked me I would've suggested we go to Universal Studios for three nights and drive to Disney World on the fourth day and then stay there for a week."

"That would've been great."

"See, that's what I mean. When we don't talk, when you keep everything to yourself, you shut me out. And the more you shut me out, the lonelier I become. I miss you, Tess. I really do. But I can't go on like this."

Tess

As we drove down the highway, I couldn't believe the words coming out of Jeremy's mouth. I didn't think he cared about planning Disney World. I assumed he was happy not to have to worry about it. But listening to his suggestion of going to Universal Studios and everything we could've done there made me realize I made assumptions I shouldn't have.

"But I didn't tell you about my idea because I knew you didn't want me to go back to work. So I thought if I had it all figured out and laid it all out for you it would show you I'd done my homework and was taking it seriously."

"I'm not going to lie," Jeremy said. "I wasn't happy about you wanting to work outside the home. I do like you being at home. But I've come to understand you need more. I'd accepted that. But my God, I had no idea you were thinking this big. Owning a tea room isn't quite the same as working part time teaching cycling class."

"I still plan to teach cycling, but I want something more. And Richard was helping me figure things out."

"Yes. And I would've liked to have helped you, too. That doesn't mean Richard shouldn't be involved. I'm grateful he's your mentor. But we could've evaluated various businesses together and, with Richard's help, made a decision—together."

I crossed my arms. "But it wasn't like I was going to go ahead and do this without telling you about it, without your approval. I need your help financially."

"Fuck, Tess. I want to mean more to you than just money. Sometimes I feel like the only thing I'm good for is bringing home a paycheck."

"That's not fair," I said.

"It might not be fair, but that's how I feel. Right or wrong, it's how I feel."

I sat back in my seat and stared out the window. Jeremy had surprised me. I had no idea he felt all these things. And I was beginning to realize just how disconnected we were. Maybe Diana was right. Jeremy might be a better partner than I ever could've imagined.

Jeremy

Tess and I checked our bags at curbside and headed for gate C1. The traffic wasn't too bad, and we had about an hour before boarding. We stopped at a bookstore on the way, and I picked up a newspaper and Tess selected a book.

"Find what you want?" I asked.

Tess nodded. "It's the latest book from Kristin Cavanaugh."

"Who's she?"

"Some romance author."

We paid for our stuff and went to the gate. It wasn't too crowded, which was nice.

"Do you know anything about the place Jen booked?" I asked.

"It's an older inn. Completely renovated, though. Sounds gorgeous. She said she booked a parlor suite and it has Victorian antiques, lace curtains and hardwood floors. She said the gardens are incredible."

"I wonder how close it is to Mallory Square?"

"A lot closer than the hotel we stayed in during our honeymoon. This inn is only a few blocks from the square. On our honeymoon, we stayed near Southernmost Point."

A memory popped up, and it made me smile. "I wonder if the dollar we wrote on and taped above the bar is still there at Captain Tony's?"

Tess smiled. "What about my underwear?"

I laughed. "I'd forgotten that you took off your underwear and pinned them to the rafter."

We laughed. I couldn't remember the last time we laughed. Maybe this is what we needed after all, to go away and be the couple we were before we had kids and responsibilities had become our new best friends.

Tess

I can still remember taking off my underwear. I was drunk and a guy sitting at the bar bet me and another girl we wouldn't do it. That's all it took for me to whip off those babies and tack them up there. Back then, there wasn't much to my underwear. It was mostly a string. But the whole bar exploded in laughter and clapped and the guy gave me a twenty. Of course, that was gone almost immediately.

I would never do something like that today. And that's a story I'll never tell my kids. Well, maybe when I'm old and wrinkled and they have to change my underwear, then I'll tell them. Come to think of it, there's a lot I won't be telling the kids. Makes me wonder if there are things about my parents that would surprise me. I never really thought about it much, but knowing Jeremy's mom is the romance author Kristin Cavanaugh, I'm sure there's a lot I don't know.

They called for us to board and, lucky us, we were one of the first on. I gave Jeremy the window seat. The plane wasn't very big. Key West has a small airport and the runway is short, so big planes can't land there, but it was a straight flight, which beat having to change planes in Miami.

I pulled out my new book from my carry-on and watched as the passengers loaded. There was a seat next to me on the aisle, and I had my fingers crossed hoping no one would sit there. I wasn't sure how full the flight was. If the seat remained vacant, I'd move over to give Jeremy and me more room.

Just when I thought things were looking pretty good the seat might stay open, an overweight man who smelled like a mixture of garlic and pine needles sat next to me. I scrunched over as close to Jeremy as I could. It was going to be a long flight.

The man, who obviously had too much to drink, fumbled with his seat belt. He finally managed to buckle it and sat back in his seat and closed his eyes.

I started to read my book, but I didn't get very far. Maybe it wasn't such a good idea to pick a book my mother-in-law had secretly written. The first sex scene I came to made me feel uneasy. Just thinking about Diana writing it scored ten on the yuck factor.

Jeremy had dozed off reading the newspaper, so I decided to get some shut eye, too. We'd be there in an hour.

Chapter 19

Jeremy

It was late when we landed in Key West, and Tess and I took a cab to our inn. We were both exhausted and fell into bed. We decided we'd talk in the morning.

I woke up earlier than Tess and walked to the grocery store, which was two blocks away on Eaton Street. The front desk clerk suggested we check out the bakery across the street from the store. "Best pastries on the island," she said.

Since our suite contained a full kitchen, I figured I'd get some bottled water, milk and cereal. And I'd stop at the bakery and buy a pastry for Tess.

Just being in Key West made me feel more relaxed. My neck and shoulder muscles didn't feel so tight, and they'd been killing me for weeks. Walking down the tree-lined sidewalk, past picket fences and eyebrow houses with intricate gingerbread made me smile.

I remember on our honeymoon, Tess fell in love with the eyebrow houses. She thought extending the roof down over the second floor windows was genius for helping to keep the inside cool. In fact, we spent one afternoon riding around the island trying to find as many eyebrow houses as we could.

Tess also loved gingerbread and Key West is home to some of the most beautiful millwork in the world— everything from orchid cornices to palm trees, parrots and even violins encircling the wide porches. Because the gingerbread on homes often reflected the inhabitants' occupations, Tess liked guessing what they did.

I remember Tess telling me that her grandmother lived in a Victorian house with lace-like gingerbread. After her grandmother died, the house was sold and the new owners, wanting the wooden house to be maintenance free, removed all of the gingerbread and covered the house in vinyl siding. When Tess saw what they'd done, she was so disappointed. "They'd turned an extraordinary house into an ordinary house," she said. "All that beauty, everything that made it unique is gone. Now, it's just like every other house. Nothing special."

I stopped at the bakery first and had a difficult time making up my mind. Everything looked delicious. I picked up a couple miniature fruit tarts, a chocolate croissant and a loaf of warm raisin bread that came right out of the oven. The chicken curry salad sandwich with apple slices looked delicious, and I made a mental note to tell Tess this would be a great place to stop for lunch.

I grabbed some water, coffee, tea, milk and cereal at the store. I would've bought a bottle or two of wine, but I couldn't carry it all back. I should've rented a bicycle at the Inn. It would've made it easier to haul things because it has a large basket.

When I returned, Tess was in the shower. So, I put the groceries away and made some coffee.

Tess

I couldn't believe we were actually in Key West. It seemed like a lifetime ago Jeremy and I had honeymooned here. But in those fourteen years, a lot had happened. We had two kids, Jeremy took over his dad's dental practice and I became the typical suburban mom, carting kids from lessons to practices and games and school functions.

I remember thinking before John was born how much our lives were going to change. Of course, what I'd envisioned was nothing like real life. Real life could be a real pain in the ass, and little cute babies grow up to be naughty and nice kids, depending on their moods. And we hadn't even hit the teen years yet. I knew that would be a real treat if Katie and John were anything like Jeremy and me. It wasn't like we were bad kids. We were adventurous, always having to find out things the hard way.

When I stepped out of the shower, I could hear Jeremy in the kitchen. I was hoping he brought back something from that bakery the clerk had told us about.

I dressed and found him in the kitchen drinking coffee and reading the local paper.

"How'd you sleep?" I asked.

"Like a puppy," Jeremy said. "You?"

"I don't even remember crawling into bed."

"I made some coffee; there's also tea," Jeremy nodded to the counter. "And I bought some pastries, too."

I smiled and put on the tea kettle to boil some water. "This place is gorgeous. Have you seen the gardens?"

Jeremy nodded. "And there's a nice pool, too. And we have our own private sitting area that overlooks the gardens."

"It's ours? We don't have to share?"

"Nope. There's a sign on the coffee table that says private sitting area for Room 122."

"Sweet."

"We can eat breakfast out there if you want." Jeremy said.

I smiled. "That would be nice."

Jeremy

Tess opened the box of pastries.

I took a sip of my coffee. "The fruit tarts are delicious."

"So you already ate?" Tess asked.

"I had a bowl of cereal and a tart. There's also a chocolate croissant that I swear had your name on it."

Tess smiled and placed the croissant on a plate she'd found in one of the kitchen cabinets. "This place has everything. Pots. Pans. Toaster. You could totally eat all of your meals in if you wanted to cook."

"Which we don't," I quickly said. "This is our vacation. No kids; just us. I don't plan on doing any cooking. The most food preparation I plan on doing is pouring cereal into a bowl and adding milk."

"Oh, that reminds me," Tess said. "We'll have to go to Pepe's on Caroline Street for breakfast. Remember how much we loved that place?"

"Definitely. Killer omelets and the best French toast I've ever had."

The teapot whistled, and Tess filled her cup with boiling water. "And they had a different bread special every day. The coconut bread was to die for!"

I'd forgotten about the daily bread special. Tess and I had eaten there the second day of our honeymoon, and it had become our favorite breakfast place.

I followed Tess outside to the porch.

"It's so peaceful here," Tess said.

I sat down on the chair next to hers. "Yeah, no kids fighting. The only thing underfoot here are the noisy free-roaming chickens."

As if on cue, a rooster must've found its way into the lush gardens below and crowed.

"Typical man," Tess said. "Makes a lot of racket over nothing."

"He's probably just defending his territory and hen. Can't blame the guy."

"Somehow I don't think we're talking about chickens anymore," Tess said.

I really didn't want to start a fight with Tess. I'd thought a lot about what she'd said, and as mad as I was she hadn't confided in me, I also knew she wasn't the only one to blame. It takes two people to make a marriage work, and I didn't think either of us was trying hard enough.

I went inside to fill up my coffee cup and get Tess more tea. When I returned she was standing at the balcony, looking down over the gardens below.

The sun peeked through the lacy canopy of green overhead and fell across Tess's long black hair, still damp from the shower. She looked stunning in her white sundress and bare feet. I realized I hadn't really looked at Tess in a long time. I mean I looked at her, but not like this, not paying attention to every curve.

I walked over next to her. I wanted to put my arm around her, but I was afraid she'd push me away.

She looked up at me, and her eyes were bright. "Thanks for bringing back the pastry. It was delicious."

"So, about that rooster wanting to protect his hen," I said.

Tess sighed. "Maybe the hen doesn't need protection. Maybe she needs a partner. You know, to make chicks and other stuff."

"Well, this rooster's done making chicks, so it must be the other stuff."

We laughed.

Tess

I sat to finish my cup of tea. "I wonder if there are any tea rooms on the island."

"So about this tea room. Why a tea room? Why not a coffee shop?"

"I guess we could do both. Tess's Tea Room upstairs and Jeremy's Joe on the first floor along with a gift shop."

"Whoa, wait! You're going too fast. Slow down. I need to catch up. That's why you were at the Bistro wasn't it? You like that property."

I smiled. "Yes. I think it'd make a fabulous tea room. But I like your idea, too. I'm serious about making the first floor a coffee shop and the second floor a tea room. Maybe the tea room is by appointment only. I could do baby and bridal shower teas, mother and daughter teas, birthday teas. The possibilities are endless. Then, on the first floor, we could run a coffee shop that's open daily. Sell coffee and pastries, delicious ones like these."

"Sounds like a lot of work," Jeremy said. "You'd have to hire help."

"I know. I have a lot to figure out. And I really do like the gift shop idea as another revenue stream. We could include specialty teas and coffees and accessories. And maybe we can feature work by local artisans."

I could tell by the look on Jeremy's face I was overwhelming him. "I'm sorry. I just get so excited when I think of all the possibilities."

"I haven't seen you this pumped up about anything in a long time. It's nice, actually. I'm really going to have to think about all of this."

"Really? You'll think about it?"

"Of course. But I can't think about something I don't know about. Now that I know, we can talk about it together."

I finished my croissant and tea. "So what do you want to do today?"

"I was kind of thinking about something touristy. Maybe the Conch Tour Train and Hemingway's House."

"And we can't miss the sunset celebration on Mallory Square," I said.

"That's a definite. I wonder if any of the performers are the same ones we saw fourteen years ago. Remember the juggler who walked on that high wire?"

I smiled. "Yes. I think I was more nervous than he was when he was up on the wire and started juggling. I expected him to fall."

"That's because you didn't have faith in him," Jeremy said. "You have to have faith, Tess. Without faith you might as well hang it up."

"Somehow I don't think we're talking about the juggler on the high wire anymore," I said.

Jeremy shrugged. "Maybe; maybe not."

Chapter 20

Jeremy

Tess finished getting ready and we left for Mallory Square to catch the closest train. We walked up Eaton Street to Duval Street, where the towering St. Paul's Episcopal Church sits on the corner. On our honeymoon, Tess insisted we go inside to see the magnificent stained-glass windows.

Tess stopped at the church. "Let's go inside. It's such a beautiful church. And peaceful."

I followed Tess through the gate. "It seems strange that such a sacred place sits right in the middle of the drinking district."

"Maybe that's good," Tess said. "It's the oldest church in Key West. I bet it's sponsored a lot of 12-step programs over the years."

Tess sat down, and I sat beside her, marveling the woodwork and windows. I had this incredible urge to hold Tess's hand. I wasn't sure what she'd do, but I couldn't help the overwhelming need I felt to be close to her. She bowed her head in prayer, and I took her hand in mine. I held it loosely, just in case she wanted to pull away. But she didn't.

We sat in silence for a few minutes until Tess looked up and asked if I was ready to go.

I nodded and our hands separated.

When we got outside, Tess turned to look at the church one more time before heading up Duval. We crossed over Caroline Street and window shopped as we made our way up the street.

I pointed to Sloppy Joe's. "I still have the shirt I bought on our honeymoon from there."

"Yes, and you need a new one. It's full of holes."

"Still good for working out in."

"That's about all it's good for. Or to be used as a rag."

We popped into Sloppy Joe's, and I bought a new shirt.

Tess laughed. "Now, maybe you can retire the other one."

"Do we want to go down Greene to Captain Tony's?" I asked.

"Let's catch the train and go to Captain Tony's tonight after the Sunset Celebration."

Tess

We bought our tickets at the festival marketplace and killed some time waiting for the next train by browsing in the sponge market. I picked up a few sea sponges to give as gifts while Jeremy looked at old photographs of sponging.

I paid for my sponges and found Jeremy. "Learn anything new?"

"The history always amazes me."

"We should head over to the train. I think I heard it pull in, and I want to get a photo of you standing next to that statue made of sponges in front of the store."

We walked out, and I pulled out my camera as Jeremy slid beside Sponge Man.

"Do you want me to take a picture of both of you?" a woman asked.

"Sure." I handed her my camera and hustled on the other side of Sponge Man.

"Smile," said the woman, snapping the photo.

"This is the only man I'm ever going to allow to come between us," said Jeremy, smiling.

"Clever," I said. "But I'm not interested in a man whose heart is full of holes. I'm looking for a man with a heart of gold. Do you know where I might be able to find one?"

Jeremy pounded his chest. "Twenty-four karat gold, baby. Right here."

I laughed. It felt good to flirt and be playful.

We hopped on the train with a boatload of tourists. "Do you want to stay on the train for the entire tour or break it up by visiting Hemingway's House?"

"Let's go to Hemingway's House."

"So we'll get off at the next stop near Truman Avenue," I said. "We might as well walk down to St. Mary's Star of the Sea, too. It's not that far from the train stop."

"What's there? I mean, besides the church?"

"Remember the hurricane grotto?"

"Oh, yeah. The shrine."

The train traveled down Duval Street past restaurants, bars and shops. A cruise ship was in port so the street, which is usually packed at night, was just as packed early afternoon. While some of the shops and restaurants had changed since our last visit, the layout and feel of the town was very much the same.

It reminded me that what you start out with is usually not what you end up with. The foundation is there, but things change over time. Sometimes for good; sometimes for bad. Sort of like the beach, which is constantly altered by the tide. Over time, the tide eats away at the beach, and you need to go back to the foundation, build it back up again.

I knew Jeremy and I had that foundation—the beach—and that we had allowed the tide of life to erode that beach. Could we restore it? That was the question. I was beginning to see bits and pieces of the Jeremy I'd fallen in love with. Bits and pieces I hadn't seen in a long time. The playful Jeremy. The sexy Jeremy. And I hadn't realized how much I had missed that. But if I felt this way about him, did he also think it about me? I was afraid to ask.

Jeremy

I looked over at Tess. God, she was beautiful. She wore her hair in a high ponytail and with her black Ray-Bans and red pouty lips she'd looked hot. I wanted to hold her and make love to her. I wondered if I'd get the chance.

I have to admit Tess was the first girl I wanted to please sexually and otherwise. I'm not too proud of this. Before I met Tess, I fucked girls; I didn't make love to them. It was all about me. I was a self-centered man whore, more interested in my own needs than someone else's. If it didn't please me, then why do it? Tess changed that. She had turned my world upside down. Suddenly, it wasn't about me and my needs, but about hers.

But somewhere along the way, things changed. I stopped listening to her needs. Not in bed, but in other areas of life. Of course, the other areas affected what happened between the sheets. Tess became less interested in sex. She pushed me away. I was starting to see that now, starting to understand how it happened. If I had the chance, I was going to make love to Tess, find a way back to where we were before kids and life had strangled us.

We pulled into the train stop near Truman Street and hopped off. "What first? Hemingway's or the Grotto?"

"Grotto," Tess said.

We walked down Truman Avenue, looking at all the wooden framed houses and gingerbread.

"I love the houses, but definitely would want more yard," Tess said. "I'd forgotten how crammed everything is."

"Guess that's why they had public parks. Places for the kids to play."

I hadn't mentioned the K word at all and as soon as it came out of my mouth, I regretted it. I love my kids, but I wanted to focus on Tess and me.

"What do you think the kids are doing?" Tess asked.

"They're in school. Katie's probably paying attention, and John's probably strategizing about how he can get the teacher to not give homework."

Tess laughed. "Like father, like son."

I had to admit, John was a lot like me, and it scared me. Not that I'd turned out bad, but the kid was always looking for a shortcut. And if he didn't find one, he'd make one. Even if it meant moving boulders the size of the earth, he'd figure out a way to do it now so it saved him later.

When we arrived at the church, Tess's steps slowed. I followed her through the beautiful gardens to the stone shrine, which was built in 1922 by Sister Gabriel and the sisters living at the convent.

We walked inside the small cave filled with burning candles and stood in quietness before the altar. It felt strange to be in such a quiet and sacred place in the middle of the day in a town known mostly for its nightlife. Funny how there are many sides of something.

Tess

We left the grotto and headed toward Hemingway's House. We were greeted at the entrance by one of the many six-toed cats.

We walked through the gardens, lush with tropical plants.

Jeremy pointed to a fat black cat drinking from a trough. "There's the urinal Hemingway took from Sloppy Joe's."

Water from a large colorful Cuban jar flowed into the urinal, disguised with tile, providing a source of water for the cats.

We toured the grounds, going around the in-ground swimming pool, built before the Navy installed a water line from the mainland.

"Remember that scene from *License to Kill* when Bond runs through the garden?"

I smiled. Jeremy is a huge James Bond fan and has all of the movies. "How do you remember stuff like that?"

He shrugged. "Guess I'm a genius."

I laughed. "Let's check out the studio."

We walked up the narrow steps to Hemingway's writing studio on the second floor of the carriage house. When Hemingway lived here, a walkway connected the studio to the porch outside his bedroom.

"Ready to head inside?" I asked.

Jeremy reached for my hand, and I didn't pull away. We walked through the door and joined the tour that was just beginning. When we walked into the room with the wall of photos of all of Hemingway's wives, I had a flashback. It was our honeymoon and the last thing on our minds was getting divorced. We were in love. Happy. And we looked forward to the new life we were building. When the tour guide explained Hemingway's marital history, I remember Jeremy whispering, "he obviously didn't have you for a wife," in my ear.

I wondered if Jeremy remembered telling me that. And, if so, was he thinking about it now and did he feel the same way? I almost asked him, but I didn't. I wasn't sure I wanted to know the answer.

We finished the tour and walked back to the train stop. When we boarded, Jeremy put his arm around me, and I wiggled a little closer. And for the first time in a long time, I felt tickly twinges, like a butterfly was busting out of its cocoon. It wasn't flying yet, but the crack was there and a wing had emerged. I wanted to be able to free it completely, but I knew it had to find its own way. I was beginning to understand that love worth keeping can't be rushed.

Chapter 21

Jeremy

After the tour, Tess and I headed to the Harborwalk and Schooner Wharf Bar to grab a bite to eat. It was Happy Hour, but we managed to get a table that overlooked the historic seaport.

"I think I'm going to get some coconut dipped shrimp with mango sauce," she said. "And an Island Cosmo Martini."

"Cosmo, eh? You must be feeling adventurous."

Tess shrugged. "Well, why not? We don't have to drive, and besides, I'm in the mood."

"Great," I said, and ordered a dozen oysters on the half shell and a draft beer. The last time Tess had a Cosmo—well, it was actually two or three—I had to put her to bed. She usually drank wine. A Cosmo meant she was willing to throw caution to the wind—something she rarely did.

A guy with tattoos for sleeves played guitar and sang on a small wooden stage tucked in the back corner. He was backed by a guy playing keyboard and another on guitar.

"I forgot how much I loved this place," said Tess, looking out toward the yachts.

I sipped my beer. "Yeah. I could get used to living here."

An older couple, both with Wonder Bread white hair, walked past us hand in hand.

Tess dabbed her mouth with her napkin. "I love seeing older couples showing affection for one another. They look like they're newlyweds, and they've probably been married fifty years."

"Do you think we'll last that long?" I asked.

"I hope so."

"You do?"

"Of course I do. I married thinking it would last forever. But things have to change between us. You see that, right?"

I nodded. "Yeah. It's taken me a while, but I see it."

The waitress came with our food, and Tess ordered another Cosmo and I ordered another beer.

Tess

I sat back in my seat. "Want any of my fries?"

Jeremy held up his hand. "I'm full."

"Me, too."

I couldn't remember the last time Jeremy and I spent quality time together. Or the last time we really talked and it not be about the kids.

I took the last sip of my Cosmo. "Ready to head to Mallory Square for Sunset Celebration?"

Jeremy flagged down our waitress, and we paid the check.

I reached for Jeremy's hand as we walked down Duval Street toward the square. We stumbled upon a guy with hairy gorilla arms and a red bandana hugging his head. He banged on large plastic buckets turned upside down. His black mutt, which looked like a mix of lab and German shepherd, lay beside him. The dog wore a pirate hat and a big pair of plastic fluorescent blue glasses. There was a basket for donations, and I tossed a couple bucks in it.

"I wonder what his story is," I said.

"What do you mean?"

"Like how he ended up here, banging on the bottoms of plastic buckets. Everyone has a story."

"Maybe he's a millionaire."

"He might just be. Who knows? Outside appearances can be deceiving. Sometimes, the people you think have the most have the least and vice versa."

"Don't get all philosophical on me now," Jeremy said.

I laughed. "Alcohol can make me introspective."

We entered Mallory Square and spotted the tightrope walker near the waterfront. He balanced the high wire on one foot while juggling.

"He's amazing," I said.

Jeremy nodded. "Yeah, I can't even balance on one foot on the ground."

We watched the juggler for a while and then watched a tumbler, a clown and a guy on a unicycle. Eventually, we ended up at the escape artist.

He picked two women from the audience to buckle him in a straitjacket and wrap him in chains. All the while he cracked jokes and mesmerized the crowd with his quick wit.

"Damn. Those are some serious chains," Jeremy said.

We watched as the performer writhed and struggled, encouraging the crowd to be more enthusiastic and louder. After a lot of banter and playing the crowd and building the anticipation, he shrugged off the chains, twisted his arms inside the straitjacket until he could stand on his head and free himself completely.

"Man, that guy is good," Jeremy said. "Amazing how he can turn what appears to be a hopeless situation into a victory."

Somehow I don't think Jeremy was just talking about the escape artist.

Jeremy

Tess and I found a waterfront spot to view the alluring sunset.

"There's nothing like watching the sun melt into the horizon," Tess said. "It's like an exclamation point to a perfect day."

"Was the day perfect?" I asked.

Tess winked. "So far. But it's not over."

I slipped my arm around her and pulled her in close. She didn't fight me or try to pull away. In fact, she laid her head on my shoulder. I loved being so close to her, smelling her citrusy scented hair. God, she was beautiful. I had an incredible urge to make love to her, to please her in ways I know I haven't in a long time. She looked so damn sexy, and my groin ached.

"I can't believe all of the sailboats on the water," Tess said. "That's something we could do. Maybe tomorrow."

"I was thinking if we went on the last snorkeling trip of the day, we'd be able to catch the sunset on the way in."

"Great idea. We'll have to book it first thing in the morning."

"I'll take care of it. I wanted to see about getting us bikes, too. I know how much you love riding around Old Town and looking at the architecture."

The crowd swelled at the waterfront. Those who didn't have cameras, used cell phones to capture the sun as it inched toward the horizon. Then, all of the sudden the sun slipped and it was gone. The crowd cheered, and Tess looked up at me. Her beautiful violet eyes and pouty lips called to me, and I bent down to find her lips and we kissed. And it wasn't like a "Hi, Honey" kiss, it was an "I want to make love to you" kiss. We both felt it and without saying anything, we left Mallory Square and headed for our room.

Tess

Maybe it was the sunset or the alcohol, but I wanted Jeremy to make love to me. I'd forgotten how sexy he was, and all I wanted to do was feel his warm body next to mine. When we opened the door to our room, we couldn't get naked fast enough.

"God, Tess. You're so beautiful."

Jeremy took me in his arms and whispered in my ear, nipping lightly. He planted kisses down my neck, and I moaned. He picked me up and gently placed me on the bed. "I want to please you, Tess. Please let me. I love you so much. Let me show you."

My insides burned with desire as he started at the top and worked his way down. Every inch of my body wanted to be physically connected to him. My hands tangled in his hair as he inched lower, past my belly button.

"So beautiful," Jeremy whispered.

I felt like I was on fire. I moaned softly. "God you're incredible."

Jeremy parted my thighs. "That's it. Relax. Let go. I want to please you."

On a scale of one to ten, Jeremy had me at fifty. "You're driving me insane."

"That's the idea."

I reached down to pull him up. My body quivered and I arched my back as he slid into me, all the while telling me how beautiful I was and how much he loved and wanted me.

"Please. I—"

"It's OK. I want to make you happy. Let go, baby. Just let go and feel me."

My entire body shook as Jeremy and I reached the mountaintop together, collapsing in each other's arms.

I'd forgotten what an amazing lover Jeremy could be, and I was sad that we had allowed our sex life to become routine and void of the deep intimacy we were obviously capable of.

I will never forget how we reconnected during our short stay in Key West. We talked and talked some more. We compromised and recommitted ourselves to our marriage and our future. Before we boarded the plane to fly home, we made a plan and a promise. The best was yet to come.

Chapter 22

Jeremy

We returned home late Saturday and told the kids we'd pick them up the next day.

Tess and I showered and fell into bed, exhausted from the flight home. I reached over and pulled her toward me, wrapping my arm around her.

"What are you thinking about?" Tess asked.

"Just how beautiful you are. And what a lucky guy I am."

Tess turned to face me, and we kissed the kind of kiss that always leads to so much more.

Tess and I talked about the tea room/coffee shop idea. She planned to make an appointment so we could both meet with her mentor, Richard. The more I thought about it the more I liked the idea of opening a business in the very place I had proposed to Tess.

Eventually, Tess fell asleep in my arms. Her black hair fanned out over my chest.

I was happy and I knew she was, too.

Tess

When we arrived at Jeremy's parents' house, Katie and John were down the street playing with some friends.

"Guess the kids didn't miss us," I said.

"Katie seemed a bit blue this morning, but when Marcia's grandkids called to see if she and John could come down, her sunny disposition returned. I think they're ready to go home."

"Can I get you kids anything?" Harry asked. "Diana baked her special chocolate cake."

"Um, that sounds good. But just a small piece," I said. "Is there coffee in the carafe?"

Diana smiled. "Just made a fresh pot."

I poured a cup of coffee and added just a smidgen of half and half. "After this week, I'll have to go on a diet."

Harry waved. "Nonsense. You look great, Tess. You always look great."

"That's what I tell her," said Jeremy, leaning over to kiss me on the cheek.

Diana smiled. "Well, it looks like maybe the trip was just what you guys needed. How was it?"

"Great," Jeremy said.

"It was better than great," I said. "It was awesome. I can't thank you enough."

Diana waved her hand. "I might be old, but I still have a trick or two up my sleeve. Now tell us all about it."

Jeremy and I took turns telling them about everything we did, except for the X-rated parts.

"I keep telling Harry we should visit Key West. We've never been there, and I'd love to see Hemingway's house and those six-toed cats."

We heard them before we saw them. The back door flew open and in bounced Katie followed by John.

"You're finally home," said Katie, running to give Jeremy and me hugs.

"Do I get a hug from you or are you too big?" I asked John.

He shrugged but walked over and hugged me anyway.

"Hey, bud," said Jeremy, rubbing the top of his head. "How's soccer going?"

John looked at his grandparents. "We didn't say a word," Harry said.

"What's up?" Jeremy asked.

"I scored the winning goal at yesterday's game," John said.

"You did more than that," Harry said. "You scored three goals, and he was asked after the game if he'd be interested in trying out for the travel team."

"Wow, bud," Jeremy said. "That's great."

"And, not to be outdone," Diana said, "Katie earned a first-place medal on the balance beam at her gymnastics competition."

"I'm so proud of you guys," I said. "Come here."

Katie and John came over and Jeremy joined us and we huddled in a big group hug. Life was looking better.

Jeremy

A week had passed since coming home from Key West and things were definitely better. I was happier, Tess was happier and the kids were happier.

"Remember, we're meeting Richard this afternoon to discuss our ideas and tour the bistro building. Then we're going to Sue and Tom's for Tom's birthday party. I can't wait to hold Daisy."

"The party's for adults, right?" I asked.

"Yes, but Daisy doesn't count."

I thought about the last time we were all together at Tom and Sue's, and I definitely didn't want a repeat. I'd also given up whiskey.

I sipped my coffee and read the morning paper. Tess sat across from me. "I've decided I'm not going to teach cycling class," she said.

I put the paper down. "But I thought it's what you wanted to do. You were so excited about it."

"You're right; I was. But I'm more excited about our business venture, and I want to devote all of my time and energy into making it a success."

"And you don't think you can do both?"

"I could, but I think my focus should be the business."

"Well, it's your call."

"I'll still go to the gym and probably take cycle classes when I can, but I won't have the pressure of preparing for classes."

I nodded. "Sounds like you have it all worked out."

"Not completely," Tess said. "But hopefully Richard and you and I will make some real progress this afternoon."

Tess

I'd been thinking about ditching the cycle class for a few days. The more I thought about it the more I realized I had to make choices and prioritize things in my life. If I was going to run a tea room and coffee shop, my workout schedule needed to be flexible. If I committed to teaching a class, there'd be no flexibility.

I just felt the timing wasn't right, but I knew it'd be tough telling Maggie.

I found her in the locker room. "Hi, Maggie."

She turned around. "Tess! Where have you been?"

I explained about Key West and how I had spent the week catching up and making some plans.

"They must be *some* plans if it kept you away from the gym."

"That's what I wanted to talk to you about."

Maggie waved for me to follow her into her office.

"What's wrong, Tess?" she said. "You're scaring me."

"I'm fine, Maggie. Really. Jeremy and I have been talking about opening a tea room. I'll be the one running it. We also might open a coffee shop on the same property. Anyway, that's where I need to focus. I don't want to teach unless I can give it one hundred percent, and I don't think I can right now."

Maggie nodded. "Well, I definitely understand. Starting a new business is incredibly stressful. You're still going to come in and exercise, right?"

"Absolutely.'

"Good, because exercising will help with the stress. And if you ever change your mind or find you have time to teach even one class a week, let me know."

"I will. And thanks for giving me this opportunity. Maybe Cole would be interested."

"Cole?"

"Yeah, he sits in the back. I sat beside him the other day, and then Jeremy and I ran into him at the builder's show. I didn't realize he's a contractor."

"I didn't either," Maggie said.

"Well, he is. Jeremy and I have an appointment with him next week to discuss a home renovation project."

"Hmm, it's something to think about. We don't have any male cycle instructors. Do you think he'd be interested?"

"I'm not sure. Maybe. But if he does it, you can count on his classes being filled. Women will fight over being able to take his class."

Maggie laughed. "Well, could be good for business."

Chapter 23

Jeremy

"I really like Richard," I told Tess after our meeting. "He's smart."

Tess nodded. "And he has a way of not making you feel dumb, even though when I started this process I was totally clueless."

We walked to our car, parked in front of the old bistro building. I opened the car door for Tess. "Your presentation to Richard was flawless. It was evident you'd done extensive research and were prepared. I'm proud of you."

The ends of Tess's mouth turned up. "You are?"

"I am."

Tess stood on her tiptoes and kissed me. A driver yelled "Get a room!" as he passed.

"Maybe we should get a room," I joked.

Tess playfully slapped my shoulder and slid into the car.

I walked around to the other side and climbed in. "And I love the old bistro building."

"Isn't the space perfect?" Tess asked. "Richard loved your idea of opening a coffee bar and gift shop on the first floor and keeping the tea room on the second floor."

I looked in my rear-view mirror and pulled out. "What do you think about asking Mom and Dad if they'd be interested in investing in the business?"

"Do you think they would be?"

"I do. Dad mentioned he was looking for something to do. Maybe a few hours a day, a few days a week, he could help out, especially in the early mornings at the coffee shop."

"That'd be fantastic," Tess said. "Then I could still see the kids off in the morning."

"Let's talk to them about it after dinner on Sunday. You can show them the presentation you showed Richard, with the tweaks he mentioned."

Tess rubbed her hands together. "I'm so excited this is going to happen."

"It's good to see you excited, Tess."

"Thanks."

"For what?"

"For being you."

Tess

So much had happened in the past two weeks. If someone would've told me I'd fall madly in love with Jeremy again, I'd have told them they were nuts. But here we were. Somehow we managed to find one another again. I knew things wouldn't always be perfect—no marriage is—but I think we made a major breakthrough and were communicating better than ever.

Jeremy still did things that upset me, like eating without a plate and getting crumbs everywhere. He joked he's practicing conservation, and I had to remind him there's no such thing in my kitchen. But the clouds that had hidden the Jeremy I'd fallen in love with had parted, and he was trying hard to be the husband, father and lover I needed him to be.

I knew I wasn't without faults, and I was working hard to do what I needed to improve. It wasn't easy, but I was making progress.

Just as I was about to slip out of the shower, Jeremy joined me.

"Jeremy! The kids."

He kissed me and the water rained down on our heads. "They're outside playing."

"What if they come in?"

"We'll hear them."

"But we have to get ready for Sue and Tom's party."

"This is part of getting ready," Jeremy said, sitting down on the shower seat. "Come on, baby. Climb on top of me."

All I had to hear was him moan baby, and I slid on top of him, wrapping my hands in his hair as he found one breast and then the other. Let's just say it was one hell of a shower.

Jeremy

We were the last ones to arrive at Sue and Tom's house.

"Here they come," Sue yelled as we walked in. "About time you got here."

Tess hugged Sue, Gina, Cookie and the others.

"The guys are in the man cave," Sue said. "We'll be down in a little bit."

She held up a tray of cheese and crackers. "Can you take this down with you?"

I took the tray and went to find the guys.

Keith saw me first. "Hey, Jer. How was Key West?"

"Great."

"Did you go to any of the clothing optional bars?" Rick asked. "I took Cookie to one when we were there the other year. Don't remember the name of the bar, but it was on the third floor. Boy was she tongue-tied when a young guy wearing nothing but shorts dropped them right in front of her and hopped on the bar stool."

"Cookie tongue-tied?" Mike said. "That has to be a first."

"It's one of the few times, I can tell you that."

We laughed.

"So Tom, how's it feel being a year older?" I asked.

"Better than it felt last year at this time when I was a year younger. I can't believe how much my life has changed in just one year. I have Sue and Chloe. My life is everything I ever hoped it would be."

"Aw," Mike said. "Isn't that sweet."

Tom threw the Nerf football at him.

"I know I sound like a sap, but hell, I'm happy."

"To Tom," Mike held up his beer. "One of the best men I know. Happy birthday, man. I hope your happiness continues to grow. You've waited a long time for the right woman, and I'm glad you finally found her."

"Truth be told, I found her a long time ago," Tom said. "I just had to wait for her to catch up."

We laughed and started a game of darts.

Gina was breastfeeding Daisy when we arrived. "Can I hold her when you're done unless there's a line?" I asked.

"Sure," Gina said. "Everyone else has held her, so you're next."

Sue poured me a glass of wine. "So tell us about Key West. And don't leave out any details."

"Do you want the clean version or the X-rated version?"

"Definitely the X-rated version," Cookie said.

"Hey, remember," Gina said. "I can't have sex for several more weeks. Not that I'd even want to put anything up my vagina right now, but still."

We laughed.

"Did you hit any of the clothing optional bars?" Cookie asked.

"No," I said, "But clothing was definitely optional in our room."

"Whoa, Tess," Kris said. "Definitely sounds like you and Jeremy are working things out."

"Or in," Cookie laughed. "Rick and I went to a clothing optional bar, and it was empty until a shirtless twenty-something showed up. He dropped his shorts right in front of me. Let me tell you he had one hell of a package. I swear, if I had a ruler, I'd have asked him if I could measure it."

We laughed.

"Rick got mad because I stared at the guy, but it was hard not to. The thing practically dragged on the ground. Okay. Maybe not quite that long, but it was by far the biggest dick I've ever seen."

"Cookie, you always make me laugh," Sue said.

I told them about the trip and about the coffee shop/tea room idea.

"So that's what you've been so secretive about," Gina said. "I never would've guessed a coffee bar and tea room. Of course, you know how much I love tea, so you'll probably see a lot of me."

"So how's motherhood going so far?" I asked Gina.

Tears welled in Gina's eyes. "I can't even describe how I feel. I'm on top of the world. Imagine finally having everything you've always wanted but never thought you'd get. That's how it is. Sometimes I think it's all a dream, and I'm afraid I'm going to wake up and none of it will be real." Gina sniffed. "The only part I'm not crazy about is the lack of sleep. It's a killer, but I know it'll get better in time. Right now, I'm trying to cherish every moment of every day."

"You're going to make me cry," Sue said.

"So are you back to shitting?" asked Cookie, injecting some humor into the conversation.

"Yes," Gina said. "No more constipation. Although I have to say after the C-section, I thought I was going to die. I had horrible gas."

"Worse than when you chew gum and swallow air and it gets trapped and gives you gas?" Cookie asked.

"A million times worse."

"Damn, Gina," Cookie said. "That's some serious high-octane gas."

"Tell me about it."

"A girl at work told me pineapple juice helps," Sue said. "She gets gas anytime she eats raw vegetables."

"Mike joked I have beautiful intestines."

"He saw your intestines?" Kris asked.

"Apparently when they pulled out my uterus and placed it on my stomach, my intestines came along with it."

"They what? Pulled out your uterus? But wasn't it attached?" Cookie said.

Gina laughed. "Of course, silly. But they pulled it out as much as they could to clean it and stitch it up. I think they also checked my bladder. Anyway, I guess that's when Mike saw my intestines."

"Rick would've been on the floor," Cookie said. "That man faints at the sight of a paper cut."

Gina burped Daisy and handed her to me. "She's absolutely beautiful, Gina."

Daisy's tiny fingers wrapped around mine and she yawned.

"You girls ready to join the guys?" Sue said.

Gina laughed. "If we have to."

"It'll be fun, I promise," Sue said. "I have some fun games to play."

"Games?" Kris asked.

"Yeah," Sue laughed. "What's a party without some dirty games?"

Jeremy

Four months later

Tess and I stood in front of the coffee bar, surrounded by our families and friends. Cole had done a fantastic job renovating the old bistro building. The bottom floor contained Jeremy's Joe coffee bar and the second floor, Tess's Tea Room. A gift shop with access from the street and through the coffee bar sold locally made products along with specialty teas and coffees and accessories and gift items.

Dad and Mom were eager to invest in the venture and Gina did, too. Dad had volunteered to open every morning, giving him something to do and allowing Tess to see the kids off to school. Tomorrow was opening day, but today was to thank everyone who helped us make our dream come true.

We weren't sure how it would go, but we weren't going to let fear keep us from trying.

I whistled to get everyone's attention. Sue and Kris made sure all of the adults had a glass of champagne and the kids sparkling cider.

"A toast," I said. "To our wonderful families and friends. Thank you for coming today and joining us in this celebration. To our mentor, Richard, who led us every step of the way. We couldn't have done it without you, man. To our contractor, Cole, who transformed this space and created a beautiful, warm escape from the busyness of life. To our kids, who spent more weekends than they care to count helping prepare for this day. To our investors, Mom, Dad and Gina, who believed in the vision and helped fulfill a dream. And, to my incredibly talented, lovely wife, who had a seed of an idea and nurtured it and made it grow. I love you, sweetheart. Most of you know I proposed to Tess here." I held up the book *Romeo and Juliet*.

"When the bill came in this book, Tess found a marriage proposal and not the check she expected. I'm giving her this book again today as a reminder of where we've been and where we're going." I handed the book to Tess. Tears streamed down her face. She opened it up. Her hand flew to her mouth. I smiled.

"What is it, Tess?" her mother said.

She took out a receipt from Tess's Tea Room. A diamond ring, much larger than the one she wore, was taped to the receipt.

Tess sniffed and read the note, "Will you marry me again?"

Tess looked at me. "Yes!"

And we kissed as the room erupted in shouts of celebration.

I slid the ring onto Tess's finger and we kissed again.

She turned around and picked up a gift sitting on the counter and handed it to me. I eagerly unwrapped it and pulled out the snow globe I'd given her in college.

"Just shake it when you want to remember I love you," Tess said.

I turned it upside down and watched the snowflakes fall.

Gina & Mike

Chapter 1

Gina

The bastard was dead.

I stared at the newspaper clipping Mom had mailed me. I'd read his obituary online, but seeing it on paper in front of me made it more real. Kind of like watching the Wicked Witch of the West melt in the "Wizard of Oz" – all the evil you loathe becoming a puddle of nothing.

Richard M. Smith, 61, was ushered into Heaven on Saturday, February 11, 2012, surrounded by his family at his home.

I'm pretty sure he went to Hell.

He was a loving husband, devoted father and dedicated coach.

He was the biggest asshole on this side of the Mason-Dixon Line. Maybe on the whole East Coast. Oh, what the hell, let's just say the entire country. You get the point, he was an A-S-S-H-O-L-E, and I hated him more than I've ever hated anyone in my life.

Mostly because he ruined it.

I grabbed my high school yearbook off the shelf in my office. Mom brought it on her last visit. She was cleaning out the basement, and it was among the things she didn't want to throw away or take to Goodwill.

I opened the book and read the message I've read so many times I know it by heart.

Gina,

To the best and sweetest girl any guy could have. You're super in every way and you mean everything to me, and don't ever forget that! You know I don't like to write because I can't express myself as well as if I would tell you but I'll try anyways. I love you very much and want our relationship to last! You're just a super girl, you care about me very much and I appreciate it because it makes me feel great inside, and I feel very lucky to have a girl as great as you. If I had to sum everything up about you in one word it would have to be amazing! It probably sounds dumb but that's the way it is. I just want to let you know that I do love you and will do anything for you that you want me to.

Love, Mike

I remember his black hair and curls. His five o'clock shadow in the middle of the day. The way his smile took up most of his olive face and the way his dark eyes danced when I walked into the room. I remember the first time he told me he loved me, and the first time we made love. Why is it that you never forget your first love? Maybe it's because it's the first person you gave your heart to, completely. The first time you were afraid to breathe for fear the moment would pass and you would miss some of the seconds. Life is seldom what we think it will be. Especially when you're seventeen and the biggest concern you have is whether someone has the same prom dress.

I ran into Mike once at the pizza shop in town. It was the day after Christmas, and I was home visiting my parents. I saw him as soon as I opened the glass door and the bell jingled. He stood at the counter, holding a baby bundled in blue. The sight washed over me like a damn wave that you never see coming until it's too late and you're face down eating sand. And just as you try to spit out the sand and stand up, you get knocked over again by the damn hot pizza smell that transports you back in time. Back to the night you ate pizza in the corner booth that still has your names carved in the wood. The night you got drunk on the six-pack you took from your dad's stash in the garage. The night you made out in the woods and fell asleep naked intertwined like pretzels under a crescent moon.

He turned and saw me and then came the smile. His white teeth seemed even whiter, his smile broader. There was small talk and more small talk. About his marriage and baby and move across town.

What happened? What happened to all the plans we had? All the nights we spent lying under the stars sharing our dreams. The kind of house we'd live in, how many kids we'd have. What their names would be. What happened to us?

Life. That's what happened. One day comes after another and another and pretty soon you realize that yesterday was pretty damn long ago and that everything you had hoped for is never going to happen. You can't control it any more than you can control that big wave from getting stronger before it nails you. All you can do is prepare and hope that when it hits, you'll survive.

And hope that the secret you've kept all of these years doesn't drown you.

"It really is an amazing perspective to be in the mind of each character and feel what they feel, see what they see."

"I highly recommend this series to anyone who loves what-could've-been stories and second chances."

"I don't know how Buffy does it, but her characters come alive and stay with you long after you've turned the last page."

" Buffy does an excellent job breathing life into her characters—giving them each a unique voice and perspective."

"The characters are very real and engage the reader from the beginning."

"The highs and lows keep you reading and anxious to see what's next."

"I hope that there will be more to the series as I want to know about the other characters!"

"Wonderfully relatable characters."

"I can't wait to read more from this author!"

"Buffy Andrews draws you in with action from the very start."

"Each page kept me turning and staying up late for."

"Buffy Andrews's works are worth taking a look at! What a great storyteller! I can't help but wish I would have thought of her idea."

"Can't wait for the rest of the series to come out."

"I highly recommend this series to everyone that wants a good read that really makes you feel a part of the book. I can't wait for more of them."

"Very well written. So real. Thoughts from the characters as the book went along kept it real and thought provoking."

"The characters in this series are consistent and you learn something new about them with every new story."

Acknowledgments

I thank God for his love, understanding and guidance and for the incredible gifts He has given me.

I thank my husband, Tom, and sons Zach and Micah, for their love and support.

I thank my sisters Dawn Beakler, Cindy Andrews and Tania Nade, for a lifetime of love and laughs.

I thank Sharon Weed for her endless encouragement, hugs and smiles.

And I thank my readers for giving me a chance in a world crowded with great books and great authors.

Facebook
www.facebook.com/AuthorBuffyAndrews

Twitter
https://twitter.com/buffyandrews

Goodreads
www.goodreads.com/author/show/
7113753.Buffy_Andrews

Website
www.authorbuffyandrews.com

Amazon
www.amazon.com/Buffy-
Andrews/e/B00EO7F1IG

About the Author

Buffy Andrews is a best-selling Amazon author of women's fiction and thriller and suspense novels. Her best-seller credits include *The Perfect Husband, The Moment Keeper, The Christmas Violin* and *A Year of Second Chances.* A two-time Pulitzer judge, she was a journalist for nearly thirty years before starting Andrews Creative Concepts. She specializes in creating viral interactive content and marketing strategies for clients worldwide. She lives in southcentral Pennsylvania with her husband, Tom.

Vote for the Class Acts couple you'd like to read about next...

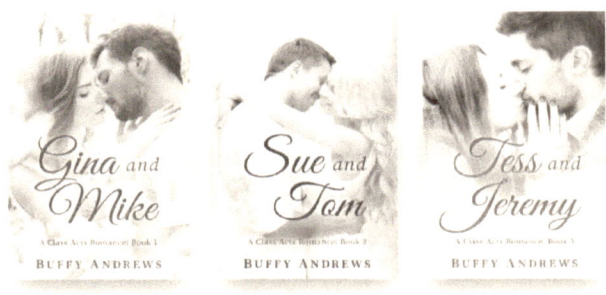

Kris and Keith

Cookie and Harry

Maggie and James

Karen and Mia

Cast your vote at http://bit.ly/35zdR9n